n
there

"You cannot hold all of the people in your hand."

A moment passed as Frane locked eyes with me. I saw a score of emotions in her gaze, among them triumph, as well as a trace of something lost long ago between us.

"In my *fist*," she said. "Fear will hold them here. And terror will keep them here." She leaned closer. "I would be afraid if I were you, Haydn. I would feel *terror*."

Jamie was clutching my arm. "Come, Haydn, before she has you murdered here and now!"

*"What have you done!"* I screamed, letting Jamie pull me back a step. "War would be madness!"

"There will be no war," Frane said, curling herself into a more comfortable position on her throne. She closed her eyes, feigning sleep, and a smile came to her face. "There will be no war."

I thought suddenly of the many empty seats in the Hall of Assembly, how few of the other tribal representatives had made their way to the hall that morning, how the few who were not F'rar looked ill at ease—afraid, even.

Outside the hall there suddenly came a horrid screech, a scream of agony that as abruptly ceased; then came another.

"Go home," Frane whispered languidly. "The Republic is dissolved. I am queen."

# HAYDN OF MARS

## AL SARRANTONIO

ACE BOOKS, NEW YORK

**THE BERKLEY PUBLISHING GROUP**
**Published by the Penguin Group**
**Penguin Group (USA) Inc.**
**375 Hudson Street, New York, New York 10014, USA**
Penguin Group (Canada), 10 Alcorn Avenue, Toronto, Ontario M4V 3B2, Canada
(a division of Pearson Penguin Canada Inc.)
Penguin Books Ltd., 80 Strand, London WC2R 0RL, England
Penguin Group Ireland, 25 St. Stephen's Green, Dublin 2, Ireland (a division of Penguin Books Ltd.)
Penguin Group (Australia), 250 Camberwell Road, Camberwell, Victoria 3124, Australia
(a division of Pearson Australia Group Pty. Ltd.)
Penguin Books India Pvt. Ltd., 11 Community Centre, Panchsheel Park, New Delhi—110 017, India
Penguin Group (NZ), Cnr. Airborne and Rosedale Roads, Albany, Auckland 1310, New Zealand
(a division of Pearson New Zealand Ltd.)
Penguin Books (South Africa) (Pty.) Ltd., 24 Sturdee Avenue, Rosebank, Johannesburg 2196,
South Africa

Penguin Books Ltd., Registered Offices: 80 Strand, London WC2R 0RL, England

This is a work of fiction. Names, characters, places, and incidents either are the product of the author's imagination or are used fictitiously, and any resemblance to actual persons, living or dead, business establishments, events, or locales is entirely coincidental.

HAYDN OF MARS

An Ace Book / published by arrangement with the author

PRINTING HISTORY
Ace mass market edition / January 2005

Copyright © 2005 by Al Sarrantonio.
Cover art by Matt Stawicki.
Cover design by Rita Frangie.
Interior text design by Stacy Irwin.

ISBN: 0-441-01236-1

ACE
Ace Books are published by The Berkley Publishing Group,
a division of Penguin Group (USA) Inc.,
375 Hudson Street, New York, New York 10014.
ACE and the "A" design
are trademarks belonging to Penguin Group (USA) Inc.

PRINTED IN THE UNITED STATES OF AMERICA

10  9  8  7  6  5  4  3  2  1

*To my brother Jerry*

# PART ONE

# CLAN

# ⊰ CHAPTER 1 ⊱

**TOBACCO WAS GOOD.**

With a pipe, a smoke ring might linger for a full minute, but I preferred cigarettes. They were not easy to come by, though, and this, unfortunately, was my last one. Which was why I stood savoring it on a cliff overlooking beautiful Noachis Terra, with my home and the capital city of Wells at my back, studying a pink sunset just turning to blue at the far horizon, and wondering what any other sky might look like.

The scientists claim the sky on Earth was once blue, bluer even than our own fringe of twilight, but I can't believe that.

There are so many things that are hard to believe—and, these days, even science provides little more than idle thoughts.

Kaylan, on all fours, moved up behind me and rested a

paw lightly on the back of my leg before pulling himself up to full height. He stood silently for a moment gazing at the horizon before speaking. I turned to study his profile: his short mane swept back behind his ears, framing his almond eyes, slitted black, always deep pools of thought; his classically shaped face covered in bare white down, soft white whiskers barely visible astride his perfect, regal nose, brown-nostriled, the downturn of his mouth that transformed itself, brightening his entire visage when he laughed—which was not often these days.

"It's hard to believe this might all be gone in a week," he said. I could not exactly place his emotions: sadness, a tinge of anger, bitterness.

"They say that war will come, and I suppose it will."

"It always has," he said, and turned his head briefly away. When he turned back he looked at me and not the horizon, and now there was defiance in his eyes.

"We have failed, you and I."

I drew heavily on my cigarette, savoring the smoke in my lungs, and then threw it to the sandstone at my feet, crushing it with my foot.

"Our marriage was supposed to prevent this. Our two clans together, J'arn and K'fry, cannot make the F'rar stop now. They are too strong. I can make them do nothing."

"But—"

"They are barbarians, Kaylan, and this is the way barbarians settle matters. Has it ever been different?" Now I turned with my own form of bitterness in my eyes. "Ever?"

He stared into the distance. "No."

Twilight had deepened, making the horizon an even darker shade of blue. The pinkness overhead was deepening to rust, letting the feeble light of the night's first stars bathe through.

"I read a picture book once," I answered, letting my tone lighten, "in which two kits travel to Earth. My mother read it to me."

He let his own voice soften. "Could you ever leave Mars, even if it was possible?"

"Could you?"

"No. You dream too much, Haydn. You always have. It's the world we have to live in, not dreams."

"You're right, of course. I'm just a spoiled girl, pampered from birth. But couldn't you dream for their sake?" I gestured a paw at my belly, already swollen with litter. For a brief moment pride and happiness, the handmaidens of hope, invaded my troubled thoughts.

"Especially not for their sake! Do you think we could raise them somewhere other than their own home? Here we might have barbarians, but we know the land. Somewhere else would be . . ." He let the thought pause in what looked like a shiver. "Unknowable."

I sighed. "You don't have to be so literal, Kaylan. It's one of the things that make us so different. A moment to dream is a good thing. Especially considering what has happened here in the real world."

Now his huge eyes were filled with alarm. "What do you mean?"

"There is word a price has been put on my head by the F'rar."

"This can't be so!"

I wished for just one more cigarette, wanted to feel the burn of sweet tobacco in my throat and lungs. Instead, I had nothing to grasp but my own words.

I nodded. "This is the word that Jamie brings me. My father was king. They see me as a threat."

"Then Jamie is a fool! The F'rar would not dare!"

"Yes, they would," I answered. I let a slight, knowing smile onto my face so that Kaylan could see it. "Come, it is getting dark. We should go in."

"Tell me what you know!"

"I only know what I learned today. Jamie came with word that the council of the F'rar clan had convened an order of condemnation. I was listed, along with Parterine and Colin. There were others, too, even lesser in stature."

"How could they do this?"

But he already knew how they could do this, and I waited for him to answer his own question: "Frane."

"Yes, Frane."

"She is evil."

I was silent.

"I will not let you go to the Hall of Assembly tomorrow," he said.

"I must go. You know that. I must try to hold back this tide. Even if it is useless."

"We will leave tonight, with what we have on our backs."

"If it were only us, I would say yes. But there are others to think of."

"Some of them are of other *clans*."

I turned to look harshly at him. "I never would have expected to hear something like that from you, Kaylan. You and I are of different clans. And many of them are friends."

He was looking at the sky; his shame was evident. "I'm sorry. It was a cruel and thoughtless thing to say." He continued to look away from me. "But I fear for you."

This, I knew, was something beyond the present argument. It spoke to something deeper—our arranged union, his love for me, my lack of it for him . . .

"Tomorrow will be all right. The order of condemnation

does not go into effect for three days. Even the F'rar would not dare to move more quickly than that. Their purpose is to uproot us and make us flee, not to murder us."

I didn't add: *At least not yet.*

"Why must you go tomorrow? If we fled tonight, it would give us that many more hours ahead of the assassins."

"A final chance, Kaylan. To try to make them all see reason, before war."

"It will be fruitless."

After a moment I said, "Yes, it will. I feel like a fool for trying. I am too young, and I have so little experience. But it is what my father would have done."

The deep blue of the horizon had crawled up overhead like a cowl, banishing the pink sky of day. The stars were out in full now, muted through the atmosphere's dust but beautiful nevertheless. There was the Pot and its companion the Ladle, and, farther south, hanging overhead like a totem, the starry figure of the Mother Cat herself, mane visible at least in the mind.

And there, in the east, like a baleful, knowing blue-green eye, was Earth, perched on the darkest horizon. I thought briefly of my mother, long dead, and that picture book. . . .

Kaylan followed my gaze, and after a moment I felt his paw slip into mine, his slender, silky fingers wrap around my own, a hint of flat claw pressing into my palm. Then he dropped to all fours, pressed his body against me before moving off toward the house—a dim, wide silhouette fifty feet behind us framed by the lights of distant Wells.

"I love you," he said.

But the words were faint, a whisper.

Almost, I knew, a resignation.

# ⇥ CHAPTER 2 ⇤

HADRIAN'S WHISKERS TWITCHED WHEN HE SPOKE; IT was a tic that had once been distinctively endearing but now was irritating beyond reason. The word *traitor* rose to my mind but I quickly banished it as unfit; *weakling* was the correct term.

At the podium he rambled on, his words booming through the Hall of Assembly. Built of solid sandstone in the ancient days, with arching support beams of the now-rare junto tree gleaming a deep, rich red as they met overhead in a domed cap of the polished bronze ten-pointed star of the Assembly of Mars, the very sight of the Hall of Assembly still took my breath away; the fact that now the hall stood half empty, with the presumed fleeing of many of its elected members, filled my heart with shame and anger.

Hadrian's basso boomed past the allotted time. I rose to speak, as was my right—and yet I was ignored.

I stood taller, and finally Frane, her figure resplendent in bright red robes, her short mane coiffed to perfection, uncurled herself from her seat and stood. She held up a long-fingered paw, nails enameled a gaudy crimson, and Hadrian immediately stopped in midsentence.

"The chair will recognize Haydn of Argyre," Frane purred theatrically. But before I could speak she added, "In good time."

"By the laws of the Assembly I demand to speak now," I replied, keeping my anger under control.

"The laws of the Assembly have been . . . suspended," Frane answered. "You should have arrived for the pre-Assembly meeting, Haydn."

"I was not told."

"Pity."

Frane curled herself back into her chair—which, I noted, had been newly adorned with rubies and deeply blue sapphires set in star-shaped gold settings, making it more throne than Assembly Speaker chair.

Frane retracted her nails and waved a paw at Hadrian. "Continue."

After a moment, seeing no point in continuing to stand, I regained my seat.

"And so," Hadrian droned on in his deep voice, "the degenerate J'arn race, as well as the rotted branches of its descendant tree, the K'fry, the Yern, the L'aag, the Sarn, and the other minor twigs of this infested, useless wood, should, in my opinion, be banished from the lands of the superior race, the only race, the pure race of the F'rar. For as we now know, the F'rar, and only the F'rar, are the mother and father of all that is good on Mars, all that is pure and sane. . . ."

I listened to this swill for another twenty minutes, and then, finally, I had had my fill of it.

Uncurling into a standing position, as tall as possible, I pointed a straight finger at Frane and shouted over the basso of Hadrian, "This is an outrage!"

Hadrian, startled from his own monotony, was instantly quiet, and there was silence in the cavernous Hall of Assembly. Even Frane narrowed her eyes.

"I demand to speak!"

Hadrian, beginning to sputter, gathered at his notes and looked to Frane for guidance. Without taking her eyes from me she said to the fat boor, "You may finish later, good Hadrian. Let Haydn speak."

She waved a languid paw at the podium, and I made my way quickly to it, passing Hadrian on all fours as he passed me, his pile of notes spilling from the pocket of his vest where they had been hastily shoved. There were some titters of amusement from the gathered Assembly members, but a sharp look from Frane quieted the hall.

I stood at the podium and clutched it with both paws. I knew how angry I looked, but there was nothing to be done.

"This entire proceeding is contemptible!" I began. I heard my words echo and fade into the back of the hall; to my further anger I watched as one row after another of the Assembly members rose to leave.

*"Sit down and listen to me!"* I shouted, and some of them stood in place to regard me; there were former colleagues in their number—friends, even—but after a moment they turned to slink away into the back of the hall.

"It seems you are losing your audience," Frane purred. She could not keep the amusement out of her voice.

"Then I'll direct my comments to you."

"Fine," she said.

"What you have done—what you are doing—will not succeed."

"Dear Haydn, it already has."

Fat Hadrian disappeared through a rear bronze door, letting it close behind him with a clang. The Hall of Assembly was empty now.

"You cannot hold all of the people in your hand."

A moment passed as Frane locked eyes with me. I saw a score of emotions in her gaze, among them triumph, as well as a trace of something lost long ago between us.

The moment passed, and she clutched her paw closed, then leaned forward with abrupt energy. "In my *fist*," she said. "Fear will hold them here. And terror will keep them here." She leaned closer, nearly uncurling from her throne, slowly opening her fist until her flat long red claws were protruded toward me. "I would be afraid if I were you, Haydn. I would feel *terror*."

"What do you—"

At that moment Jamie, my page, appeared behind me, face blank with fear. He put a paw on my arm.

"They want me to take you."

"Where?"

"I would go home if I were you," Frane said, and I turned to confront her.

My voice was a whisper. "What have you done?"

*"Terror,"* Frane answered, her eyes slitted and bright with hatred.

Jamie was clutching my arm. "Come, Haydn, before she has you murdered here and now!"

*"What have you done?"* I screamed, letting Jamie pull me back a step. "War would be madness!"

"There will be no war," Frane said, curling herself into

a more comfortable position on her throne. I saw that its
seat had been brocaded in deep blue, with threaded pictures of ancient cats, wearing the crest of the family of
F'rar. As she stretched up momentarily, before settling
down into a more comfortable position, I saw that her own
figure was brocaded in gold in the center of the seat.

She closed her eyes, feigning sleep, and a smile came to
her face. "There will be no war."

I thought suddenly of the many empty seats in the Hall
of Assembly, how few of the other tribal representatives
had made their way to the hall that morning, how the few
who were not F'rar looked ill at ease—afraid, even.

Outside the hall there came a suddenly horrid screech,
a scream of agony that as abruptly ceased; then there came
another.

"Go home," Frane whispered languidly. "The Republic
is dissolved. I am queen."


"THE ONLY REASON YOU AREN'T DEAD IS THAT FRANE
wants you to see what she has done, because of your father.
Because of . . . you. But she will have you killed later. Parterine and Colin are already dead."

"Kaylan . . ." I said.

Jamie would not look me in the eye. "I tried to tell you
about our movement months ago, but you wouldn't listen.
Now it is your only chance to survive."

"Frane doesn't know about you."

"If she knew, I would be dead. We would all be dead."

"I must go to Kaylan."

"You must not go home, Haydn."

"No one will prevent me."

I looked at this youngster, this boy I had known from

his birth, this page I had taken for granted for so many years, in a new way.

"You knew of all this," I said. Around us, the streets were swept clean of citizens, the tall buildings of Wells shut against the daylight. The sun overhead was a small bronze coin in a high pink sky. The day was as still as death. I thought briefly of the crowds I had seen around the outside of the Hall of Assembly, the red-shirted thugs surrounding one or two citizens, some of whom I knew—the flash of curled daggers against the light of that bronze coin, the screams as Jamie hurried me past, not letting me stop to help.

After a moment Jamie answered. "Yes, I knew of most of it. All of our group did. But we did not know that today would be the day. And we did not know that Frane would act so . . . decisively."

"That's a well-chosen word, Jamie."

*If you murder your foe, there can be no war.*

He smiled briefly, perhaps at my bitterness. I followed him through a narrow alley between two tall sandstone buildings; as we emerged into a square I heard a far-off howl of pain. I turned, my instinct to help, but Jamie took me by the arm and begged me to move on.

"We must take back ways," he explained; "there are redshirts who no doubt would consider it a badge of honor to kill you, no matter what Frane's orders."

We continued in this fashion, making our way through Wells by less-traveled corridors. There was not a soul to be seen on the streets. As we passed through the bazaar section, the widest avenue of Wells, closed always to all but foot traffic, I was struck dumb by the silence, the abandoned or unopened stalls, their canvas covers flapping in the wind. Pink dust swirled in empty streets where thousands of citizens would normally be jostling one another at this time of day; the sound of laughter and the happy cries of children had been replaced by eerie, dry silence. I paused to look behind us; there, in the distance, at the end of the avenue, stood the old Imperial Tower, the seat of government when Mars had been ruled by monarch instead of legislature. It was a magnificent structure still, its slender, sand-colored columns topped by spired towers, its central bulk, darker in color, rising even above these to a massive belltower whose four-sided clock face, white as polar snow, dominated the entire city. As I watched, the hour struck, sending a hollow, deathly deep *bong* over the empty seat of power. Higher yet above that clock tower sat the old imperial throne room, gilded in gold and bronze. I had no doubt that at this moment Frane was ascending the ancient stairs to take her place on the most magnificent of thrones. I had curled up in that throne once, when I was yet a kitten, placed there by my father. I could almost see the last king, the first true republican of Mars, looking down at me grimly, a strange light in his eyes, his lips pulled back in what I thought was a smile, though his voice held no humor.

"Take pleasure in the feeling, young Haydn," he had said to me, snatching me from the throne even as I became comfortable, and setting me on the floor, "and pray that you, or anyone else, never feels it again. It is the mark of death. . . ."

Barely two months after that day, my father lay dead in a pool of his own blood, victim of an assassin's dagger.

Jamie's fingers were curled around my arm, hurrying me on.

"We must go—"

"Kaylan—" I said again.

"I beg you once more not to go home," Jamie answered. "There is a safe house waiting, and transportation out of Wells."

"As I said, I will go home first."

Something hardened in his eyes. "Very well."

Overhead an airship passed, its sleek ovoid shape, painted blood red, slicing the sky. Something small and black dropped from it as it floated over the city, and a moment later there was a flash of light brighter than daylight, followed by a thudding boom that I felt in my chest. This was followed by a rising mushroom of gray-white smoke.

"That was the Hall of Assembly," Jamie said in shocked awe.

My gaze drifted back to the clock tower, the throne room above it. "She won't need the hall now that she is queen."

"She is not the true queen."

I ignored his comment.

We moved quickly. My thoughts were only of my husband now. We reached the city's outskirts and then suddenly left Wells behind. I glanced back to see the lazy black smoke of new fires dotting the pink city behind us. I turned away. A thousand times I had walked this road, which led to the highlands above Wells; its cobblestones were well known to my steps. But now the climb was a long one.

"A final time I beg you—" Jamie began as we topped the rise that led to the scattering of homes overlooking the far plain of Noachis Terra. It was one of the most beautiful of all places on this part of Mars to live, and my steps became faster when my home, wide and serene, magnificent among the few homes up here, rose into view.

As we reached the black wrought iron front gate Jamie

tried to stop me once more, but I pushed him aside and went through, my ears barely registering the familiar creak of the rusted hinges. In my nostrils was the faint hot smell of midday dust—and something else. . . .

Incongruously, and though my throat was dry, I longed at that moment for a cigarette.

All was silence, and the front door stood wide open. Inside there was a greater silence, and I found Kaylan in our sleeping chamber, on his side, seemingly asleep with his face away from me. It was only when I approached that I saw the stains of red at his throat.

Jamie was there to steady me, and whispered in my ear, "You must come now. I feel Frane will change her mind and have you killed before we can get you away."

I stood still, even as he clutched me, and then I moved closer to the bed, bending gently to kiss Kaylan, feeling the soft brush of his whiskers on my face.

"I am so sorry," I whispered gently, so that Jamie could not hear me. "So sorry I did not love you more."

I stood then and turned, and let Jamie lead me away from that place.

# ⊰ CHAPTER 3 ⊱

**SOMEWHERE IN DARKNESS . . .**

I awoke with my back aching, and a cramp in my side. For a moment I feared for my litter, and brought my hand across my swollen belly. But the moment of fear passed and I realized that my backache and cramp were due to the sleeping position I had been forced to assume in the hollow, dark, close false bottom of the wine wagon that bore me. I could hear the red liquid sloshing against the rounded sides of the huge cask above me, and the faint smell of tannin tickled my nostrils.

As I was instructed, I gave a rap on the side of my prison, counted to four, and gave another rap.

There was no answer, and for a moment a new kind of panic filled me. What if the wagon had been waylaid, or we had been found out . . .

To my relief, an answering, resounding *thwack* sounded on the outside of the cask, just above my head.

The wagon slowed, then stopped. In another moment I felt the vehicle shiver as the driver debarked.

There was a faint grunt and then a square of darkness opened in front of me, letting in cold night air.

"You require something?" a gruff, obeisant voice said. The face was ravaged, one eyesocket empty, a missing ear, a long, deep scar, even in the darkness visible like a dark paint stroke from the scalp to the lipline.

"No, Xarr, I only wish to inquire about our progress."

"We have been stopped twice. Once at the city gates, a thorough search, and again by F'rar henchmen, on the road between Wells and Bradbury. The second time they were interested only in the wine."

I saw him smile, his head haloed by distant pinpoints of stars.

"And you, Xarr?"

The smile widened. "I am interested only in the wine, too."

"Ah. That accounts for your breath."

I heard movement, and Jamie's sleek head appeared beside the driver's.

"What's wrong?" Jamie asked anxiously. "I was nearly a kilo ahead before I turned back—"

"Nothing's wrong, Jamie. I merely needed to know our progress and to stretch my aching back. I would like to get out for a few minutes if possible. The curved bottoms of these carriers are most uncomfortable, especially for one carrying a litter."

The young page's voice became even more anxious. "We cannot stop here. And you cannot leave your hiding spot. We are still in much danger. There may be F'rar watching us from the hills. We could be accosted again at any moment—"

"I understand. It was wrong of me. Then we must proceed at once."

Almost before I had said the words, Jamie nodded, and the square of night was closed up. I heard Xarr climb with an *oof* back up to his seat. In a moment the wagon rolled on.

I curled first one way, then another, but could not find comfort.

I thought of my own selfishness, and of the many others like me who now lay dead in the streets of Wells. Parterine and Colin, my father's old friends, and so many others . . .

Seeking to cure my aching back, I thought of my own dead husband, his throat cut as casually as if he had been a slaughtered chicken.

I thought of all these things and then, finally, I slept.

THIS TIME WHEN THE SQUARE WAS REMOVED IT WAS filled with brilliant sunlight.

Jamie's face appeared, less anxious.

"How do you feel this morning?"

"I would like to throw up," I answered honestly.

Then, mustering as much dignity as I could, I leaned out of the opening and did so in front of my page.

To his credit, he merely stepped back, then waited patiently for me to finish.

"It must be hard bearing . . ."

I let him help me from the hiding place. "It was not morning sickness, Jamie." I waved a paw back at my former prison, which, I now saw, was even more decrepit than I had thought. "It was the damned smell of bad *wine*. . . ."

"*Good* wine!" the gruff voice of Xarr chimed in, and now I saw the ravaged-faced cat approaching us unsteadily on two feet.

"You drink too much of your own wares," I said.

"If you looked like me," he laughed, brushing a paw across the ruined left side of his face, "you would do the same!" He stood regarding me with an amused look. "So this is little Haydn . . ."

Jamie interceded. "That's enough, General." He moved toward the vintner, who merely brushed him aside with a swipe of a paw.

At the utterance of the word "general" my attention focused more sharply on the ravaged-faced cat.

"Let me finish, whelp," the vintner said to my page.

Jamie, finding himself on the ground, was about to speak when Xarr looked down at him, his eyes hardening. *"I said, 'Let me finish.' "*

Jamie was silent, and Xarr looked back up at me. His face was an unreadable mixture of drunkeness, cunning, cruelty, and a dozen other emotions lost in his ugliness.

"These," he said, brushing his paw along the line of his scar, even more horrific—a red, deep welt turned over on itself in its bad healing, from his lips up past his missing eye and lost ear—"I earned for your father." His voice suddenly became even and cold. He tweaked his nose, his other eye, other ear. "I would lose the rest for you. That is all I have to say."

Abruptly, he turned and staggered away, leaving me open-mouthed and Jamie standing once again, brushing himself off.

*"That was General Xarr Fealdon?"* I said in wonder. "I had no idea . . ."

Jamie said, "Xarr is a common name. I thought you knew."

"I thought he was long dead. I last saw him the day my father was murdered. He disappeared—"

"He did not disappear. He was thrown out of his generalship and joined up with us. Many old friends of your father are with us. We are well prepared."

"It's time you told me everything, Jamie."

"Soon," he said. "There are others you must see."

As if on cue, the camp we found ourselves in came alive. I noticed that the tents had been pitched on a high, flat bluff, surrounded on all sides by miles of semidesert. There was one road in, a gentle slope with no cover on either side. In the distance the rim of a crater glowed like a wall against the early sun. The sky was pink and clear and cold.

I thought immediately how vulnerable this place would be from the airships.

"We have spotters in the distant hills, and antiair batteries at the four horizons" a strong, clear voice said behind me.

I turned to see someone I knew—someone I had known. . . .

"Kerl—"

"You shouldn't whisper," he said, smiling. "Your whisper makes me feel as if I am still far away from you."

"Kerl—"

I felt suddenly lightheaded, and had the horrible, distinct impression that I would collapse into my own vomit.

There were strong hands on me as I fainted, and I heard Kerl order, "Take her to my tent."

Then, again, I slept.

• • •

I AWOKE WITH THE IMAGE OF THE SUN BURNING
through the tent overhead.

Late afternoon, I judged by the sun's height.

I felt rested and refreshed. The cushions beneath me
were as soft as the bottom of the wine cask had been hard.
Scented petals floated in a water bowl on the floor nearby.
An overhead fan, its blades made of red junto wood, turned
lazy and slow in one corner, moving the dusty air.

The tent flap was thrown aside, and Kerl was there.

He had not been a dream after all. . . .

"I waited for you to rouse," he said.

He entered, and let the flap fall behind him.

He was taller than his brother, and broader. Where Kaylan had been elegant and slim, his younger brother was
solid as stone. His mane was thick and luxurious, his features chiseled but saved from hardness by a soft mouth. I
had been in love with him nearly my whole life.

"It was cruel, the way you left," I said simply, holding
his gaze.

"When my brother was picked—"

"Over your mother's objections, and your brother's
own," I reminded him.

"True. But my father, as usual, got his way. . . ." His
gaze drifted off for a moment.

"Yes. And he paid for it with his life, along with many
other senators."

"True again. But he led me to understand that there
were reasons why I must leave when I did."

Some of my evident hardness melted. "Then it wasn't
your idea?"

He looked at me levelly. "No. But there was more going
on than you ever knew, Haydn. This usurpation by Frane

was coming for a long time. The republic was doomed the day your father was assassinated."

"And I was naive enough to think I could help keep the republic together."

I noticed that he had not taken a step closer to me.

I could contain my anger no longer. "And you left without saying a word to me!"

"It had to be done. Already there were plots within plots. When you married my brother, it was already evident the republic would fail and the monarchy would return. Our goal was to make sure you became queen, not Frane. You are the legitimate heir to the throne. We needed time to ensure that."

"Then my happiness was sacrificed to buy you *time?*" My voice rose to a near-hysterical pitch.

He took the verbal blows and stood unbowed. "Yes," he said. "Your marriage to my brother was a bandage to keep the republic together for another year." He looked away. "But it still wasn't long enough."

"And you and I—"

His voice dropped to a whisper, and he took a step back. "You and I . . ."

He turned quickly and was through the flap before I could utter another word.

WHEN I EMERGED FROM THE TENT, WASHED AND composed, twenty minutes later I was told that Kerl was gone, had ridden by horse to check the northern fortifications. The day was lowering toward twilight, and the camp was readying for the night. I counted a few more than forty heads, and there were less tents than there had been earlier in the day.

"Are we breaking camp?" I asked Jamie, who appeared next to me like a shadow. The cook fires had been started, and the succulent odor of roasting poultry filled the air. I suddenly realized how long it had been since I had eaten.

"No. The camp is splitting. You and I will stay here for one more day at least."

At my table Jamie seated me and then moved off, making way for Xarr, who seemed to rise out of the twilight like a fat spirit.

He sat down opposite me, a little unsteadily.

"Tasting your wares again, General?" I asked with amusement, and a great deal more respect than I had previously shown when I thought he was just a drunken vintner.

He grinned. "My lady, I am properly potted most hours of most days. Occupational hazard, I'm afraid." His face momentarily darkened. "The things I've seen in the past two years . . ."

A steward appeared with a flagon, and filled Xarr's cup, and then attempted to fill mine.

"Is that the same stuff that came out of Xarr's wagon?" I asked.

He bowed slightly. "It is, ma'am. We've been looking forward to its delivery."

I kept my paw over my cup. "Having lived with it in such close quarters, I'll forgo."

"As you wish."

He bowed again and started to move off, until Xarr grabbed his arm and removed the flagon from it.

"Leave it with me," he said, and the steward started to protest. He thought better of it when the general growled loudly at him.

Xarr chuckled hoarsely as the shaken servant made off.

Seriously, I said, "Tell me where you have been, Xarr."

"Me?" he said, feigning levity. "Why, I've been to the north, the east, the west, just about everywhere, little Haydn."

I patted my bulging middle. "Certainly not little anymore."

"You'll always be little Haydn to me," he said. "When you were just a kit, I remember you never wanted to frolic like the others. Always wanted to learn the sword, or history."

"I'm afraid we've had too much history lately, Xarr."

He leaned forward, and I knew for sure now that behind the veil of insobriety the same hard, solid man I had known when young still resided. "Not nearly enough history, you mean. Not by a long shot."

"What do you mean?"

He leaned back and tilted his cup to his lips. He belched. His look was hooded and grave. "I've watched you from afar, I have," he said. "All your machinations and speechifying in Assembly. I watched it and studied it. We all did."

"While I bought time for you?" I said, recalling my conversation with Kerl and letting some bitterness leak through.

"That's right," he said. He paused to drink again. "And you made very fine speeches, you did." He chuckled grimly. "Completely useless, but, yes, very fine."

My anger rose, but he continued, ignoring it. "Your father, before he was murdered, got what he wanted, as he often did. He was the finest man I ever knew. And when he abdicated, he made sure that the monarchy was replaced by something better for the people, and without a drop of blood being spilled, except, eventually, his own.

"But he was wrong in thinking that it would work. He had brought it on too soon. We tried to tell him, but he wouldn't listen. The clans weren't ready for it, and neither were the common people, who only think in terms of clan, anyway. While he was alive no one dared say anything against him. But after he was butchered, those of us who knew the republic were doomed began to work to see that if the monarchy was reinstated, the legitimate line continued and you were crowned queen."

He pointed at my food. "You aren't eating, little Haydn."

Suddenly I was no longer hungry. The odor of burned poultry made me want to vomit again.

"Go on," I said.

Xarr paused to eat a bit and drink much. "I see I have your attention. So, where was I?"

"A return to monarchy. Me as queen. So you knew all along that Frane would usurp?"

He was drinking when I said this, and nearly choked.

"*No!* We knew the F'rar, and Frane in particular, were a great danger. But we had no idea how strong Frane had become, or how bold she would be. I'm ashamed to say we were caught unawares. But now, little Haydn, we will do what we must to make sure you are returned to the throne."

I was silent so long that he finally said, "This does not please you, having so many willing to fight and die for you?"

"I've spent my whole life trying to ensure that the monarchy never returns," I answered. "My father taught this to me from the moment I could sit still long enough to listen! He sat me on the throne once, just to show me how horrible a place it is."

Xarr was staring at me over his cup. He had stopped drinking.

"Oh, don't worry, little Haydn. You need do nothing. They mean for you to be little more than a figurehead, anyhow." That strange mixture of cunning and a myriad of other emotions had returned to his face.

I was speechless with rage. Xarr continued to look at me in the lowering darkness with his grin.

"I can see your father in you now, little Haydn. Can you imagine someone telling him he would be nothing but a pretty bauble to hold up in front of the people?"

"If I were ever to be crowned queen," I said, measuring my words, "it would only be to ensure the restoration of the republic."

"Ah, I have no doubt. But first you must become queen. Oh, the wheels within wheels, and your friend Jamie always in the middle of them. He was the first to see that the monarchy would return. He saw far ahead of the others that the Republic would fail."

"And Kerl?"

"Kerl is the best fighter I've ever known. But he did as he was told," he said, giving his hoarse chuckle. "Much the worse for him, since he had always been in love with you as much as you are with him. Or so he's told me many a night over a cup or ten of my wares. Jamie thought your marriage to Kaylan would not save the Republic, and he was right. But he was outvoted by others, many of them dead now. And so Kerl's brother, being eldest, had to marry you. For a brief moment there, it was thought that Jamie was wrong, that your union with Kaylan might form the glue to hold the republic, and the clans, together after all. And then your father was butchered last year. . . ."

He stared off into the lowering sun, which made his

savage features shadowed with a kind of sadness and nobility.

When he continued, his voice was lower, still gruff, but had lost all of its effects of alcohol. "Everything unraveled after that, little Haydn. And quickly. It had been hoped that if the Republic started to fail, then the Assembly would turn to you because of your father, and because of your union with Kaylan. You would have been the legitimate choice to mount the restored monarchy. But the F'rar were more treacherous, and had been harder at work, than we knew. We were forced to retreat and regroup, while the F'rar, and Frane in particular, only became stronger. And then, suddenly, there was nothing we could do but run like dogs. . . . "

He turned his face on me in the near-darkness. "We failed you, Haydn. We knew nearly a month ago of Frane's plans." He laughed bitterly, reached for his cup, and then drew his hand away. "We still had a few spies worthy of the name. One of them was my son."

I held my breath. "Your son . . ."

He nodded, staring now at his cup. "I did not drink so much a month ago. He was a page, like young Jamie, and just as good if not better at being a spy. An aide to Senator Paterine."

"I remember him," I said. "But I never knew him as your son."

Xarr nodded, and toyed with the stem of his cup. Abruptly he drew it to his lips and swallowed what was within in one gulp. "My only son and heir. And we had to leave him in Wells City."

"Why wasn't I told any of this?" I asked. Anger was beginning to build in me, gently, as the first swell of a storm.

He slammed the cup down and nearly hissed: *"Because it was necessary."*

I tried to overtake his anger with my own. "How dare—"

Again he slammed the cup down, and this time it shattered in his hand.

"No, madam, how dare *you* presume to know what you could not know! Do you know how many women and men have died in your name already? How many will yet die . . ."

He held himself back, but I caught him.

"Tell me everything you know," I said.

"I cannot."

"And if I order you to?"

He laughed, pulled my own cup across the table, and put it to his lips. "You have not been crowned yet, little Haydn."

My rage was held in check by the strange timbre of his words. "Xarr—"

He swept his paw out in dismissal, and I saw that it was bleeding from the cut glass of his goblet.

"There's blood—" I began.

"There will be much blood," he whispered. "I apologize, Haydn. I have already said too much."

He reached for the wine flask, and it was evident now that he was very drunk indeed.

"Let me help you," I said, reaching for his bloody paw.

Another gesture of dismissal. "You've already done enough." He put both paws on the table and started to push himself unsteadily up. Then he abruptly let himself down again.

"Remember this," he said, his voice a slur now. "And remember this always. I would die for you. I would die for you this minute. But I think you are too young. You may have your father in you, but he has not roared forth yet. All your swordplay and history as a kit did not prepare you for this. You have not lived, little Haydn. Your father kept you too safe. We all did. And now, I'm afraid, it was a disservice. I'm sorry. You are not ready. . . ."

His head lowered slowly to the table, and in a few moments he was snoring, his massive, ugly head resting on his paws in the midst of broken glass.

As if on cue, Jamie was there.

"Did you hear any of that?" I asked.

"Enough."

"We must talk, Jamie."

"Yes, we must."

"Help me with him." I rose and went around the table, lifting Xarr's head gently away from the table while Jamie cleared the debris away.

"Help me carry him to his bed."

"Lay his head back down on the table," Jamie said.

"It is cruel."

"It is what he would wish. He will be ashamed if he finds himself in a bed of cushions that he did not stagger to himself. In the morning he will awake and find his wine nearby. It is what he would want. Ever since his son was killed he has been like this."

I started to protest in a louder voice, but Jamie gently but firmly forced me to lower the vintner's head back into the thick nest of his waiting paws.

Xarr snorted once, then settled into a rough sleep suffused with loud snores.

"As I said, it is what he would want," Jamie said, walking away.

I caught up with him, and the two of us proceeded to the edge of the bluff. Something dark stirred nearby, and my breath caught in my throat until I realized that it was a figure, a guard stationed nearby wrapped in a cloak against the night's chill. Jamie gave greeting, and was answered by a grunt, and we moved farther away. I could see another guard huddled like a rock not far away on the other side.

The new night was clear and cold, the pink of twilight fading like gauze on the western horizon into purple and then, higher, harsh black. Stars dappled the sky, pale above the pink sunset and then sharp as knife points overhead. With a pang I remembered such nights, and standing thus with my husband, at my home at Wells. If such times had not been filled with love, they had at least been suffused with warm affection.

"I am missing Kaylan at this moment," I said.

"Not Kerl?" Jamie said, almost slyly. His transformation from young, waiting page to something more had become complete. I wondered what other secrets he harbored.

"I will not speak of that," I said. "What I will do is ask you if my presence here is a danger."

He laughed without humor. "A danger? We are in mortal danger each second we spend in this place. Those hills out there, the rim of that crater"—he stretched his paw out and swept it broadly from left to right—"are suffused with our troops and those loyal to you. There will be a great battle here within the week that will transform our planet and perhaps seal its fate." He turned and looked grimly at me. "Danger? I would say it is complete."

"What have I done to bring this on?"

"Nothing," he said. "It was inevitable. But when it is over, you will be a great queen." His tone was almost obeisant.

"Apparently for the moment I am to be a figurehead, nothing more."

His gaze was on the distant hills, the invisible army.

"You are astute, and so is Xarr, in his own way. This is how it must be. You are much too valuable to lead an army—"

"Enough!"

He shook his head. "It has already been decided."

"A figurehead . . ."

"Yes."

I sighed. "Then I must change their minds."

Another humorless laugh. "Tomorrow morning at dawn you will be back in Xarr's wine cask on wheels and heading farther north, toward the equator. We have safe stops all along the way. If Xarr doesn't drink his own supply dry before we get there, you will be out of harm's way. And if all goes well, soon you will be on the throne."

"What if I refuse to go?"

His laugh was even drier. "You have no choice."

"Did you lose anyone in Wells, Jamie?"

He turned to look at me, his eyes widening slightly. "You *are* astute. Much more so than I ever saw you on the floor of the Assembly."

"Who?"

"My sister, my mother. Frane made sure I knew about it, only because of my closeness to you."

"I'm so sorry."

"Yes." He turned to stare at the horizon.

"If I had only known . . ."

He was silent.

"Do you know why my husband, Kaylan, was killed, Jamie?"

"Because he was your husband."

"No. Because he was Frane's true love."

I watched Jamie's mouth open in astonishment. "This explains why Frane allowed you to go home. She wanted you to see with your own eyes what she had done."

"Yes. My husband loved me, Jamie, but I did not love him. I'm sure this was common knowledge. But how many knew of Frane's love for him? She had loved him ever since they were kits. She loved him to the point that she would slaughter him, when given the chance, rather than let another have him. What does that tell you about her, Jamie? About the depths of her ruthlessness? Do you think there's a lesson there?"

"Then it's also true that she let emotion overrule reason. She should have had you killed in the Hall of Assembly. Instead, we were able to smuggle you out of Wells."

I turned to him in the darkness and let my voice harden. "Perhaps if I had not been treated as such a kit, a tool, by your secret movement, I might have been of more use to you. Can you imagine what might have happened if Frane had been allowed to marry Kaylan, instead of me? We might not be in the position we are now. Or at least would have been able to buy more time." My anger rose to my lips. "But I was *used*, instead of consulted, and here we are.

"But I will not be used any longer. From this moment on, Jamie, I am not a figurehead."

He had not taken his eyes from the horizon, but then he nodded. He began to say something, but then stopped. Finally he said simply, "Be ready to travel at dawn."

He walked away, leaving me to the night, and the hard, cold stars, and the morass of confused thoughts that filled my head.

# CHAPTER 4

THE CONCUSSION OF A BOMB WOKE ME FROM MY sleep.

There had been the brief beginnings of a dream: my father and I in the throne room, and he was lifting me onto the throne, which I saw had no bottom as he dropped me onto it. And I watched him recede, staring down at me calmly above as I fell and fell into a bottomless hole . . .

And then I woke up.

As I uncurled from sleep, still feeling as though I were falling, Jamie burst into the tent.

"We're being attacked!" he said. "We must get you away immediately—"

"I'm staying," I said simply. "I will fight with the rest."

He was looking from me to outside. In the cut of the tent opening I saw a plume of bright smoke shoot straight up in the near distance, followed by a thudding *boom*. The ground beneath me shook.

"This is not what we thought," he said cryptically. "Again they move too soon!"

"Jamie," I explained, "I'm not leaving. I let you spirit me out of Wells, but not this time. I'm going to be more than just a figurehead."

He looked at me and then nodded. He advanced toward me with his paw out. I thought he was going to take my arm in friendship, but at the last moment I saw the needle he held, and then it was too late.

"This is for your own good, my queen," he whispered, and then, amid the sound of thunder and shouting, I went away.


I AWOKE IN THE HORRID, HOLLOWED-OUT CASK WITH the nauseating smell of red wine in my nostrils. There were sounds outside, raucous laughter, but the wine cart wasn't moving.

I banged on the side of the cask as before, and the laughter immediately ceased.

There came no answering *thwack* from Xarr.

Hands were moving over the outside of the cask. I realized that whoever was out there hadn't known I was inside.

The panel in front of me moved partway open, stuck, and then was yanked aside.

A strange face outlined by darkness peered in.

"So?" it said.

Rough hands reached in and pulled me out.

I was dropped onto the ground like so much baggage. I counted three dimly seen figures around me. The closest, who had pulled me from my hiding spot, was staring down at me with his head cocked at an angle.

"What is this?" he said in a strangely inflected voice. The accent was rough—northern, I thought.

One of the others kicked at me and said, "Yes, what?"

"Is it wine?" the third said, and the other two laughed. "Perhaps we should drink it?"

The three figures stiffened as a fourth appeared, throwing two of them aside.

"What do you find?"

The figure who had pulled me from the cask pointed to me but said nothing.

"This, O Mighty!"

"What are you?" the one who had been called "mighty" said to me.

Slowly I got up.

When he saw my swollen belly, Mighty's demeanor changed in an instant.

"She is with kith!" he roared at the others. "And you treat her like this, you maggots?" He swatted at the nearest of the three, catching him on the head with a great blow.

"We didn't know—!" a second said as a similar blow struck him, sending him to the ground.

"I apologize for my fools," Mighty said to me. And then he bowed.

"You are of the Yern clan," I ventured tentatively.

He stood straight and proud. "Yes!"

"Nomads from the north?"

"We take no council from other clans, and give none ourselves. We are vagabonds, and proud to be so!"

"You were never represented in the Assembly . . ."

Again his demeanor changed. He looked at the opening in the cask, strode over to it, and poked his head inside.

He came back and stared me in the face, first with one eye, then the other. His breath smelled of fish and Xarr's wine.

I suddenly thought of Xarr.

"What happened to the driver of the cart?" I asked.

Mighty's companions laughed. One of them made a slitting motion across his throat.

A chill went through me until Mighty said, "He was nothing. A F'rar, and a scrawny one at that. He mewled for his mother. So we sent him to her." He paused and grinned at his companions. "Assuming his mother's dead, of course!"

They laughed, as much out of fear for their leader as at what he said.

"F'rar . . ." I said.

Mighty stood tall again. "Yes! There was a great battle near the crater called Galle. We watched it from the far rim. And when it was over we came down and helped ourselves.

"Scavengers," I said, mostly to myself.

"Vultures!" he roared. "Who drop down upon their prey like death itself!" The other three stepped back. For a moment Mighty drew his hand back but then regained his composure as his eyes focused once more on my belly.

"A man who strikes a woman with kith should die, and quickly," he said. "But you try my patience. Tell me who you are. Or have you spent your whole life inside a wine cask?"

The others laughed weakly at the joke.

I considered telling him my real name, though I doubted it would mean anything to him. These were nomads who had never been yoked to any Martian law, monarchy or republic. When we were children our parents used to scare us with them. They were vapors in the night who appeared, plundered, and disappeared in a breath of wind.

"I am an important person," I said simply.

"I gathered as much. Either that or a wine steward gone to extraordinary lengths to guard his wares. And where there is import there is money, no doubt."

"I would be handsomely ransomed."

He nodded. "I have no doubt of that, too. And you shall be ransomed, and handsomely, at the falling of the year."

That was months away. "If you are to ransom me, it cannot wait till winter!"

He grunted a laugh. "We follow no calendar but our own. Come, you may eat with me. Food is prepared."

Without waiting for my reply, he strode off, nudging the nearest of the three minions aside with a growl.

Seeing no alternative, I followed.

The camp was not a large one. I counted three tents, one larger than the others. As I passed the opening I saw two women within, overdressed in silks and jewels. They stared at me with baleful eyes.

"Come! Eat!" Mighty said from his fire nearby.

He waited for me to sit on a pillow, then sat opposite me. He was handsomer in firelight, not as old as I assumed. His features were almost aquiline. The nose was broad and his whiskers thick.

He dipped a paw into a pot that straddled the fire, drew something to his mouth, then barked a command and one of the minions appeared and carried the pot to me.

"I prefer utensils," I said.

He laughed, and slapped his knee with a paw. "And I prefer to be king of the universe! Alas! Neither of us attains what we prefer!"

My hunger overcoming my reticence, I scooped some of the glop within the pot up with one paw, and managed to spill half of it bringing it to my mouth.

"No!" Mighty laughed. "Like this!"

The minion scurried back to him with the pot and he proceeded to instruct me how to properly eat with my paws, scooping it gently into the hollow of his palm, then bringing it almost elegantly to his lips.

I had to admit that the stew, if that's what it was, was very good.

"You like F'rar stew, then?" Mighty asked after I had eaten my fill. He began to laugh as my eyes widened in horror.

I began to retch and stood up.

"No! No!" He continued to laugh, urging me to sit back down. He waved his paws. "It is only poultry!"

He waited until I had regained my seat to announce, "We will have F'rar for dessert!"

Again he laughed, and then added quickly, "We are nomads, but not savages. Please do not think of us as so."

"I . . . had my doubts," I said.

His grin widened. "I am sure you did! And now I will tell you about the battle today."

My interest heightened. "Please."

With his paw, he drew a line in the air, and then, higher, another, and then another. Then he lay his paw flat above the third line.

"This is where your people stood on the high bluff," he said. "We have excellent spyglasses, and saw it all." He moved his paw down to where he had drawn the second line. "And your people had their outer defenses here, to the rim of the crater." He traced the original, lower line, again.

"And here were the F'rar, beyond that line." He took both paws and bent the line upward and around.

"A flanking maneuver," I said.

He nodded vigorously. "Yes! And a good one. There were many more F'rar than your people. The F'rar, being stupid, waited for dawn to break. Your defenses then went to work, and did well for a time. But after a while they were overwhelmed."

He hunched himself closer to the fire. "Then the main attack began. It went on for a long time, almost two meals' worth. Your people had picked the bluff well, and they defended it with vigor. The airship attacks, I think, eventually made the difference. That and the fact that the F'rar had fifty times the ground attackers as your defenders. And then, of course, there were betrayals."

I must have looked surprised, because he laughed.

"Yes! There are always betrayals! With my own eyes I watched through a spyglass as two of your defenders on the crater rim took money to abandon their posts. They were later killed by the F'rar. I'm sure there were others."

"Tell me more!"

"So eager!" He laughed again. "Eventually the F'rar got into the southern defenses of the bluff. But before that happened, I saw a curious thing, what looked like a wine cart being ridden off to the east. A band of F'rar chased it, and eventually they overtook it. And I said to myself, 'I must have that cart!'"

I must have looked pensive, because he leaned closer to the fire and said, "What are you thinking, Ransom? That will be my name for you, I believe, since you refuse to give me your own."

I nodded absently, thinking of General Xarr.

"And now," Mighty announced, "we will have that dessert! My women are excellent cooks!"

"Your . . . harem?"

"Of course! Every Yern of import must have one. And the women fight to be part of it!"

"Don't the women ever . . . object?"

His smile faded. "What is this silliness? Are we going to discuss Yern savagery again? These are the ways of my people, how it ever was!"

My own ire was building. "And if the women were to object?"

"They would be beaten! And rightly so!"

"This is just?"

He threw his paws up. "I should have known better than to discuss things of import with one like you. You are not Yern! You do not understand!"

"I don't suppose you consider me part of your harem now, do you?" I said defiantly.

"Who are you, that you speak to Mighty like this!" He stood, angry. "You are a guest, and one with kith! Of course you are not part of my harem! But tonight you will sleep with them!"

He stalked off, and in a moment one of the women I had seen in the large tent appeared out of the shadows.

"You must come with me." She had a sly smile on her face.

When I started to protest, she said, "Now. He is very angry."

I followed her into the tent, where the other woman was making up a bed of pillows in one corner.

"You will sleep here," she said in the direct tones of a head servant brooking no discussion. When she turned to regard me she had the same sly smile on her face.

"Very well," I said.

The two of them retreated behind a curtain deeper into the tent.

"He will be angry, but it will be worth it," one of them said to the other, and then the two of them tittered.

I lay down on the bed they had made me, and immediately noticed an odd smell, which only grew in intensity. I began to gag.

Almost immediately Mighty appeared, and when he saw me his face flushed in anger.

"What is the meaning of this? Who told you to sleep with the dogs?"

I got up, disgusted. "And your dogs are not trained to relieve themselves outside?"

"They do what they wish. As do I."

He threw open the back curtain to reveal the two cowering women behind it. In a moment the curtain dropped, and I heard the sounds of paw striking flesh and pitiful mewlings.

I was about to push open the curtain and intercede when he reappeared, flushed with his exertions. But his ire had subsided.

"They will wait on you hand and foot from now on," he said, in an apologetic tone. "I should have known something like this would happen. The ways of women . . ."

He must not have liked the look on my face, because he stormed toward me, his anger rising again. "For your information, Ransom," he said, "my mother headed this tribe before me. She had her own harem—of men."

He stalked out.

In another moment the two chastened women appeared from behind the curtain. The older one approached me, eyes downcast, but I caught the sullen look of smoldering hatred on the other's face as she held the curtain open.

"Please," the older one said, indicating that I should enter the rear chamber.

They followed me in, and the younger one bent to arrange the pillows, now luxuriously heaped in one corner, of what had undoubtedly been their own beds.

As they left, the younger one lingered before letting the curtain fall behind her, and fixed me with her murderous stare. I saw that the older one was already rearranging the dog's bed into two separate sleep areas.

I slept that night with one eye open.

# ⊰ CHAPTER 5 ⊱

THE NEXT MORNING I AWOKE EYE TO EYE WITH A DOG.

He was not a large one, which surprised me. He was obviously used to being kicked because he jumped back, giving a single hoarse bark, when I opened my eyes. There was no reason to like dogs, and this one would obviously not change my mind—it was dirty and fearful and, I could already tell, spoiled and needy. My father had briefly owned one, which promptly ran away the first time it was unleashed. As pets, dogs were, as far as I could tell, burdensome; as companions, unpredictable; and as protectors, useless. In short, I didn't like them.

The creature, making a piteous sound in the back of its throat, sat on its haunches and then tried to advance on me again. I brushed it away.

"Go," I said.

"It is his house, much more than yours!" the booming

voice of Mighty sounded from behind the curtain. He sounded in a good mood. "May I enter, Ransom?"

I arranged myself and sat up. "Of course."

"It is a beautiful morning," he said, throwing the curtain aside, "and we must soon be away. You will breakfast with me?"

"Do I have a choice?"

He smiled broadly. "You have every choice at your disposal. You may dine with me, or not dine at all. You may fly, if you have wings. Or you may make a friend of a dog."

Through all of this his pet had sat crying and barking hoarsely, waiting for his master's attention. When it came, and Mighty looked at it and held down a paw, the beast jumped up joyously and licked at it, running its tongue over the outstretched fingers.

"His name is Little One. Do you not find their needs to be curious?" Mighty said. He looked down at the dog with unabashed affection. "It is said that they are content to be subservient, unlike our own species."

He looked to me for confirmation, and I nodded. "I have heard that. I have also heard that they are stupid." I cringed as the creature had left off debasing itself in front of its master and now advanced on me, tongue lolling.

"He likes you. And that is significant, because he likes almost no one."

As if on cue, the younger of Mighty's harem stuck her head into the tent. The dog immediately turned, growling angrily in the back of its throat.

Mighty surveyed the scene and laughed. When the woman had withdrawn, he turned to me and said, "I had a little chat with Myra this morning, about her plans to slit your throat. I'm sure you may have sensed her displeasure with you. Suffice it to say there will be no further offense to you. Besides, you will have your own tent tonight."

"Thank you," I said, letting some of the sarcasm in my voice reach him.

The dog had crept to within a foot of me, and put out a paw as if to shake my own.

Tentatively, I took it.

"Friends for life!" Mighty roared, laughing. He turned away, and the dog instantly left me, to trot along behind him. "And now, breakfast!"

He looked back at me and smiled. "Or not?"

"I'm hungry," I replied.

"Good. I will see you at the fire, then." He looked down at the dog. "No more need to share a bed with Ransom, Little One!"

THE MORNING HAD DAWNED CLOUDY. IN THE DISTANT west I could see a building dust storm. Overhead there were water clouds, but not heavy enough to drop rain. The air smelled tart and moist.

"You said we would be heading north?" I asked as I sat down to dine with Mighty.

He nodded. "It is our season to spend in Terra Meridiani. I have family there, many cousins and uncles and nieces. You will like it, though it is mostly infertile and inhospitable. Especially to one like yourself, used to the lushness of the south."

"I have seen pictures of the region. Does much grow there?"

"Very little." He smiled. "It is a good place to be left alone by the F'rar and other bothersome clans."

I said nothing, but ate, dipping my paw into the pot,

which was this time suspended between us over the smoldering fire from the night before.

"You are already very good," he said, admiring my eating technique.

"Hunger is a good teacher," I said. "I held a bit of the flavorful mass up for his inspection. "F'rar?" I asked sarcastically.

He chuckled. "No, dog."

I hesitated, then waited for him to confirm his joke.

"It really is dog," he explained. "We breed them, as cattle. Little One is an exception. He is the best breeder among them, and so has escaped the knife. And once he found his way into my affections . . ."

He shrugged, and smiled at me.

"Dog . . ." I said, losing part of my appetite. "I had heard there were some clans that ate dog . . ."

"We are not the only ones. The Ferals, of the extreme north, are known to dine on nothing else. And of course the Baldies, who will eat anything . . ."

At the mention of that other childhood ogre I must have shivered.

"You have never seen a Baldie?" he asked.

"No."

"They are interesting creatures. Insane, but interesting."

"So I've heard."

He laughed. "Where *have* you been in your life, Ransom?"

"Wells City, and Lowell City, and a few summers at Hellas, at one of the lakes."

"Playpens all!" he scoffed. "You have never been anywhere outside these comfortable places?"

"No."

"A pity! My mother used to call city people 'bum wipers.'"

"Without civilization, what do you have?"

"Me!" he laughed. "The rest of the world! Oh, there is much for you to see in this world, Ransom. The great northern volcanoes, the Ocean of Utopia. Perhaps you will see some wonderful things with me!"

I nodded absently. Despite my distaste, I had finished my meal.

Mighty belched. "That was fine! And now we go!"

As we had talked, the camp had been breaking up around us. I saw now that there were more than just the three male companions and the two women I had seen before. Other tents dotted the near hillsides, and these were falling like deflated balloons as I watched. The sky overhead had darkened. The dust storm that had been at the western horizon looked ominously closer, curlicues of pink sand touching ground and sky.

"We will have interesting weather before the day is out," Mighty said. He rose and clapped his hands.

Two men came running; one of them took the pot and ran off while the other smoothed out the remains of the fire until there were no signs that it had ever been there.

Wagons were being loaded, and a tribesman had already climbed into the cab of Xarr's wine wagon. Its horses snuffled impatiently, no doubt sensing the coming storm.

I briefly thought of the ravaged-faced general who had vowed to die for me, and wondered what had happened to him.

"Do you wish to travel in your hiding place, or with me?" Mighty asked, standing beside me. He indicated two bridled horses nearby.

"I don't ride well," I said.

"And I have no time to teach you now. Ride in the wine wagon, then, but up top, with Horn."

Horn, one of the three figures I had first met the night before, appeared and bowed. He held out his paw, and I took it.

"My *lady,*" he said.

Mighty laughed at the sarcasm, and made as if to swat Horn, who cringed away from the feigned blow.

"He mocks you," Mighty said. "Her name is Ransom," he instructed Horn, who nodded.

"Come then," Horn said, turning away. When I reached the wagon, he was already mounted, and let me climb up by myself.

Without a word he snapped the reins, and the wagon began to roll.

Soon we were a caravan, and the day darkened.

AT WHAT I JUDGED TO BE NOON BY THE LIGHT OF THE sun, which shone like a sour shadow through the thickening clouds, our kilo-long line of carts and horses came to an abrupt halt.

Without a word, Horn, who had been less than communicative since we set out, threw the reins aside and climbed down.

He joined the others, including Mighty, flanked by the two women, who walked a good distance from the caravan and formed an impromptu circle.

I had heard of this ritual of the noon but had never witnessed it.

Soon, on all fours, heads bowed to the ground and, eyes closed, they began to chant, a rhythmic mewling that was nearly borne away by the wind before it reached me.

It was very dark now, and the wind had begun to pick up. Tickles of sand swirled around the wheels of the wagon. Dust devils played up from the ground before vanishing like ghosts. The highlands were behind us. We were heading into more desolate territory, with only cactus and an occasional plot of tall yellow grass to break the dusty terrain.

I looked back the way we had come. It was still brighter there. I might be able to outwalk the storm.

Stealthily, I climbed down from the wagon and crept off.

Not thirty paces later, the dust storm closed in around me, and I was instantly lost.

Knowing that the winds had been coming from the west, I headed east, with their back to me.

With any luck, I might find my way to the highlands, or at least to another, more hospitable clan.

I walked, on two legs and then on four, and then, after what seemed hours, I could walk no more, and thought to rest for a moment, my face to the ground. . . .


"SHE HAS COURAGE, I'LL GIVE HER THAT. IT IS THE most foolish sort of courage, of course, but I do admire it."

Someone laughed, a woman's voice, and I opened my eyes to find myself in my tent, with bright sun blazing through the opening.

"Did I dream?" I said, trying to get up and then wincing in pain.

I was wearing a loose garment. My own clothes were gone.

One of the women, Myra, the younger of the harem,

was standing beside me. She had not lost the look of burning hatred in her eyes.

Mighty bent down over me and smiled. "You have very little pelt left on your back," he explained. "The wind shredded your garments, and then began to shred you. Luckily we found you as soon as the storm lifted." His grin widened. "Two days ago!"

"Two days . . ." I tried not to move, but sought to return Mighty's look of defiance. "How far did I get?"

"Not very. A few kilometers. And I have very little understanding of why you were heading west."

"I was walking east, with the wind at my back."

He barked a laugh. "The winds in these storms can change in a moment! Not like those baby storms you have in your playpens in the south! I imagine you were headed to each of the compass points for an equal time."

I groaned. I suddenly very much wanted a cigarette.

"Do you have any tobacco?" I asked.

"No. It is against our faith. And it was very bad of you to sneak away during the noon ritual," he scolded mildly. "There are many gods you may have angered."

"Who exactly do you worship?"

"Why, the sun, of course! At least during the day. And the two moons at night. And then there is the Blue Lady, of course."

"Blue Lady . . ."

"In the night sky. The wanderer among the stars."

"Earth."

He scoffed. "I don't know this name. To us, she is the Blue Lady. There are many tales. . . ."

He noticed my discomfort, and turned to Myra. "Bathe her," he ordered. "And apply ointment. And see that she is well fed." To me he said, "Where were you going, Ransom, that you wanted to head east?"

I was silent.

"Ah," he said. He bowed. "Until later, then."

After he left, Myra turned to me, holding a wet cloth and said, with smiling malice, "This will hurt. Turn over."

It did hurt.

WHEN THE SUN WAS SINKING, MIGHTY CAME TO SEE me again. We were now alone. He pulled up a stool to my bedside and looked at me seriously.

"I am beginning to understand you a little, Ransom," he said. "But you must not try to run away again. It will only bring you grief. And not from me.

"We must travel tomorrow, which will bring pain to you, I'm afraid. We will travel through some interesting, and dangerous, places. Others would not treat you as I have."

"The equator?"

"Eventually." He stroked his whiskers thoughtfully. "The fact that you tried to get away does not bother me. It was to be expected, and showed courage. But the foolish nature of the act does bother me. That and something else . . ."

I waited for him to continue, but he stood up.

"We will speak of these things later. Suffice it to say that we are being pursued."

My heart leaped.

"They are not your people," he added, "so do not rejoice. They are F'rar. They want you very badly, Ransom. Another might give you to them, to protect his own. Honor, of course, does not allow me to do that. Also, I hate the F'rar. But their ardor troubles me. We have already as-sassinated two of their sentries, and still they come."

He stretched. "Ah, well. They are F'rar, so they are stu-pid. And once we get to the middle lands, they will not dare follow." He grinned slyly. "And you will be worth even more, the longer we keep you, eh?"

I said nothing, and he left.

MYRA APPEARED WITH FEARFUL EYES IN THE MIDDLE of the night and shook me awake.

*"Get up!"* she hissed, nearly pushing me out of bed. "Get up or we will all die!"

Painfully, I climbed out of bed, and the girl threw a heavy cloak around me.

"Follow!" she ordered.

She nearly dragged me out of the tent. I could feel her fear. I began to be afraid myself. I stumbled out of the tent behind her and saw the sky full of lights, F'rar airships landing all around us.

"Come!"

I moved with her, keeping low to the ground, nearly on all fours, as she was. Somewhere in the near distance a gunshot sounded, followed by the hiss of arrows.

We moved away from the camp, down a sandy slope and among a stand of bushes.

"Down!" she ordered, and I threw myself flat on the ground as a spotlight stabbed down from above, skittering off to our right and away.

"Move!"

We scrambled on a fair distance, and then the girl sud-dcnly ordered, "Get in!"

I was shoved ahead of her into a dark opening.

Like a crab, she scuttled in after me and then reached up and pulled something flat and wide over the opening. Huffing with the effort, she crouched down beside me and hissed into my ear, "Say nothing!"

I nodded in the darkness, and we sat and waited.

It was not a long wait. Above there was a sound like thunder on wheels, and many barking voices. The sounds became impossibly loud.

Suddenly I heard someone shout just over our heads, "Damn these sand rats! Where in hell did they go?"

"I saw them from above, sir. They were right here."

"If they were right here, where did they get to? Did they melt into thin air?"

"We'll keep looking, sir."

"You do that. Did we get anything out of the prisoner?"

I felt my companion stiffen beside me.

"Nothing. You know the way these creatures are. She died without speaking."

"Damn!"

The sounds, the figures, moved off.

My companion was shivering, weeping softly beside me.

In the dark, while we waited, without speaking, I put my arm around her and pulled her close.


I MUST HAVE SLEPT. THREE TAPS ON THE TRAPDOOR above us woke me.

My companion was already awake. She sprung up and instantly pulled the door away, revealing bright sun.

"They are gone," Mighty reported. His face was grim.

"Ena!" my companion cried, climbing out of the hole and falling into Mighty's arms.

Idly he held and petted her. "Yes," he said. "She is being prepared for burial. It is almost noon. Come, Myra."

Myra collapsed. "Ena! Ena!"

Mighty supported her, and looked down at me as I climbed from the hole. "They caught her as she was making her way to her own hiding place," he said. "Rather than reveal the spot, she let them take her. They burned her, and then they put her eyes out. And she said *nothing*." There was a mixture of grief and pride in his voice.

"Oh, Ena!" Myra cried.

I stood, and took the weight of Myra from Mighty. "Let me help her," I said.

He nodded, and he looked at me in a new way. "I am beginning to think that taking you was very bad luck for me," he said. "This is nothing against you, you must understand. But there are bigger things going on on this world of ours than I imagined."

"You are right," I said.

"We will talk," he said, and walked away, leaving the care of his harem girl to me.


ENA WAS BURIED AT PRECISELY NOON, WITHIN THE circle the remaining caravan members made.

I was not allowed to help form the circle, but stood just behind Mighty, who explained everything to me.

"The body is purified by the sun. The sun is a good god to be buried under. He will protect her in the next world. The moons are not so favorable, because they can be tricksters. It was a good omen for her to die when she did."

The body lay sewn into a sack made of tent cloth next to a dug hole. After prayers Myra left the circle and annointed the sack with oils and aromatic herbs. Some of the odors wafted to my nostrils: jasmine and oleander, and the heavily rich perfume of cactus oil.

After Myra's ministrations, there followed what I at first thought was an extended moment of silence, but I saw that the members of the circle were mumbling under their breaths.

When it was finished, Mighty, the last to stop speaking in a low voice, explained to me, "The announcing of her sins." I saw him give a slight, knowing smile. "She had many."

Then the members of the circle collapsed on the body and lowered it into the ground, covering it and smoothing the area so it looked as though they had never been there.

"Ordinarily," Mighty explained to me after this was done, "we would leave a mound so that the sun could find the spot, but since we are being followed, this cannot be done. For the next three days during noon service we will remind the sun of her location." He looked up at the small golden yellow coin in the sky. "He will not forget. She had her faults, but she was a good woman."

He looked at me curiously.

"What is it you believe, Ransom?"

"You mean my religion?"

"Yes."

"That is a difficult question to answer."

"On the contrary, it is the easiest question to answer."

"I was brought up to believe in the One," I replied. "But sometimes it has been difficult to believe even in that."

"Why so?" He looked genuinely puzzled.

"Because of the way things are."

"You mean the evil in the world?"

"Yes."

"All the more reason to believe in something. Even if it is only the silliness of one god."

"Perhaps you are right."

"We will speak of these things again, but now we will hide, and then tonight we will travel. And we will continue to travel by night, and hide by day, until we are out of danger."

"I had no idea you had built hiding spots," I said.

I saw for the first time since that morning a little of his humor return. "Oh, I am full of surprises, Ransom."

"Yes, you are," I said to myself as he strode away, and I beheld the five bodies of F'rar he had captured and killed, then hung head down and naked on long poles on a distant hill to tell his enemy that he could not win.

# ⇥ CHAPTER 6 ⇤

**A MONTH PASSED. EVEN THOUGH WE APPROACHED**
the equator, it grew colder, due to the changing of seasons.
In effect, the southern winter was overtaking us.

I learned to wear their clothes, out of necessity. I became accustomed to their ways. My back had healed, and
Myra's ministrations were the cause. I knew she was proud
of her work. A taut understanding, if not respect, had
grown between us. Occasionally I still saw daggers in her
eyes—but I had yet to see one in her paw.

I puzzled over her relationship with Mighty. In the past
weeks we had been joined by others of Mighty's clan.
Often they appeared at night, like wraiths. More than once
I had awakened in the morning to find that our camp had
doubled in size during darkness. Among these newcomers
were others of Mighty's harem. I awoke one morning to
discover that one of the younger wives had managed to

crawl into my bed undetected and slept beside me. And she snored! Which may have made it much more an indication of the ease I felt in this camp, that I would sleep so deeply.

My belly grew. It grew inexorably, and I could feel the life within me. By the movements and occasional kicks, I determined that there were at least two kits, possibly more. I know I glowed, because those around me glowed when they looked at me.

Mighty maintained his polite but intense interest in me. I knew that he had sent spies hither and yon in search of my identity, but never did he reveal any of this, or what they might have found, to me. He was a very shrewd card player, even if I had to explain to him what card games were.

"We have no need for this rubbish," he said, throwing down his hand of Jakra the first time I tried to teach him. It was a cool evening, and fires had been permitted. We had seen no signs of the F'rar in nearly two weeks. But I knew Mighty had eyes out there, watching, listening.

I laughed, and showed him my own winning hand: three Vestas, the figure of a broad old feline with abundant whiskers staring seriously out of the face of the card.

"You have no need because you have no skill!" I teased.

He did not take this well, and turned back to the cards.

"Deal another . . ."

"Hand?" I offered, still teasing.

"Yes! Hand! Deal me out another!"

As I dealt, he concentrated and spat, "We will see who has no skill."

He won the next four hands.

"You see," he explained as we took a break from the game and sipped gemel tea that Hera, the latest, snoring member of his harem, brought. I had grown a fondness for this tea, which was robust, by no means weak. I noticed the young thing would not meet my eyes, since, I had been informed by Mighty, she thought she was crawling into bed with *him* her first night in camp. "It is like this. When I call this . . . card playing"—and here he waved his paw in dismissal at the pile of discards on the ground between us—"rubbish, I mean it in a literal sense. Rubbish to my people is things that are irrelevant to survival and the everyday. Even our kits would not indulge themselves in games like this. We draw our pleasure from constructing and preserving, not"—again he waved his dismissive hand over the cards—*"that."*

"But it's enjoyable!" I protested.

He shook his head. "Enjoyment is in . . ." And wordlessly he spread his hands to take in the black sky overhead, the thousands of stars, the planets, the night air, the planet.

In my weeks with this man, I now knew what he meant.

"I must ask you," he said, turning his attention back to the cards. He flipped a few of them over, exposing the faces of the great Martian feline composers. "These names you give to the faces . . ."

My eyes widened. "You cannot read?"

I saw the beginnings of anger. He stabbed at the cards with an outstretched clawed finger. "No."

"But why not?"

Before he answered I did it for him: "More rubbish?"

His anger immediately receded, and he pointed to the cards again. "Who are all of these bum wipers?"

I riffled through them, and brought out a particular one: a tall, proud feline with an abundant mane and kindly eyes. I handed it to Mighty. "This is a composer named Haydn. She was a musician, as were all of these."

He nodded as he took the card. "I wondered why the game was called Jakra: music."

"It is said that Haydn was named after another composer, one of the Old Ones," I explained.

"These Old Ones are rubbish to me, also," he said, throwing the card down onto the pile. "If they are unknown they might as well be ghosts, to frighten the children with at night. They are not real."

"They were real," I insisted. "It's just that we don't know much about them. Only that they were here before us."

He looked startled. "What is this? You say that these Old Ones were born of Mars before the Yern and the other clans?"

"They were here, and then they disappeared. And we don't know why."

He stood, kicking the cards aside, and became furious. "You spout nonsense! This cannot be! There are the gods, and the clans. Nothing more!"

I spoke calmly. "These are the beliefs of my people, just as you have yours. We believe in one god, and that the Blue Lady, as you call her, is another planet that circles the sun, just as Mars does. The other wanderers, Bright One and Little Bright One, also are planets. And we believe in the Old Ones, because we have evidence that they were here."

He was holding his head with his paws. "Enough! I will hear no more of this sacrilege!"

That night he burned two special fires facing west, and a particularly noxious incense was added, which, I am sure, he made sure drifted directly into my tent to keep me very awake.

●   ●   ●

THE NEXT MORNING HE WAS, I THINK, APOLOGETIC, though he did not, of course, apologize.

Over breakfast he said, "You will be very interested in our destination today."

"How so?" I said, still rubbing my eyes, and trying to clear the smell of chicken offal and cactus spice from my nostrils.

"You will see," he said, cryptically. Then he added, "As for last evening, I have decided that I have my beliefs, and you have yours. There is nothing I can do about that."

"Thank you."

"Even if your beliefs are those of a dog," he said, and got up and strode away.

We decamped soon after. Our caravan had grown to more than twenty wagons, nearly a hundred individuals. It was as if Mighty were picking up a nation while he traveled, which was, of course, very nearly the case. His people were scattered, I gathered, in an area some two hundred kilos wide and nearly five hundred long. Since we had started in the extreme south of his territory, we were gathering them up as we went along, like a farmer harvesting grain.

The territory was starker, and yet in its way as beautiful, as that in the south. Long stretches of near-desert were punctuated by oases of fertility, green and yellow patches that burst out of the pink-red scenery like dabs of color on a canvas. The sky was brighter here, a thinner pink but with many wisps of cloud. And it held less craters, more hills, and the occasional peak of a ridge or low mountain.

There was not much game to catch, but Mighty did have his herd of dogs, which ran along at the rear of the caravan barking and complaining and, usually, less one member the next day. They bred fairly quickly.

Horn, my companion in the wine wagon, continued to be, as from the beginning, maddeningly uncommunicative. He seemed content to hum to himself all day, or to point out things that held no particular interest. "There's a bluff I used to play on when I was a kit!" he would exclaim, but when I asked him about his boyhood, he would say nothing. Or, "Look at that line of junto trees!" to which I would say, "What about it?" which would leave him shaking his head, returning to his humming.

About midday this day Mighty rode back to us, leading a second horse. I had begun to learn to ride, but was still better off on the wagon.

"Come with me," he said, and Horn immediately ceased his humming and stopped the wagon.

I climbed down and then up onto the steed.

"Where are we going?"

"I told you there was something you would like. It is complete rubbish, but you will like it."

I followed him, and we headed to the west away from the caravan, up a long, seemingly endless hill. I noted that we were not alone; as usual, lining our route there were guards and sentries, whom Mighty did not even bother to acknowledge.

After an hour of this upward trot I said, "Are you sure there's something worth seeing ahead?"

Without turning his head he answered, "You are like the kit who, in the wagon, keeps asking, 'Are we there yet?' "

Before I could say anything he added, "We will be there soon."

After another hour he announced, "Just over this rise."

We topped the second of two high hills we had mounted. I stopped a moment to look back. The caravan was invisible on the plain below us. A mist had settled far below.

"We are high," I said, noting the thinner atmosphere.

"Yes," Mighty answered, and pointed ahead, over the rise, as my horse settled in beside his.

I gasped, and for a moment held my breath before whispering, "Oh, my . . ."

Mighty sat up straight on his horse, beaming. "I knew you would like it!"

Below us, in a bowl formed by our hill and others surrounding, was a mythical place from my childhood:

One of the places of the Old Ones.

The series of tall red smokestacks gave it away immediately. The myth was that they were always in threes, and here were three sets of three stacks, as well as smaller sets of three around the perimeter of the site. Some of the stacks looked as if they had been through war. There were many buildings, some of them crumbling, some at least partially intact.

"Can we go down?" I asked.

"Of course. I suppose you will insist that the Old Ones built it."

"They did."

He shook his head and rode on.

The path down was a treacherous one, and more than once my horse slipped on rocks and pieces of debris that had been scattered by whatever calamity had befallen the site. There was a metal gate and fence at the bottom in a woven pattern, but torn and blasted apart in places. We entered through a wide-open area where the fence was completely gone.

A building loomed ahead, silhouetting three massive

chimneys behind it, one of which was unscathed. The other two had been nearly cut in half.

The building, made of blocks of sandstone with many broken windows, had a gaping hole in one wall. Mighty pointed to it and said, "We can go in there. But you must leave your horse here."

We dismounted, and I followed him.

I passed broken pieces of machinery, a pile of broken wall.

Inside, it was gloomy and cool.

I noted the many switches on the pitted walls. There was electrical cable everywhere, the skeletal wrecks of huge, unknown machines—large vats, a perfectly square riveted metal monstrosity that rose nearly to the ceiling, where a series of catwalks, most of them partially destroyed, crisscrossed under strings of broken light fixtures.

"Most of the buildings look like this one," Mighty said, shrugging. "But I had no doubt you would find it interesting."

"Do you know what this was used for?"

"Rubbish, no doubt," he answered, kicking at a dusty coil of frayed cable.

"There is a legend . . ."

He laughed, the sound sending a booming echo through the building. "There is always a legend, Ransom. For everything. That does not make it true."

I was half listening to him, wandering on ahead. There were a series of rooms cut into the far wall, and I made my way to them, skirting two tall pillars studded with dials and switches.

"We cannot stay here forever, Ransom," Mighty said behind me.

I noted the impatience in his voice but went on.

The first room was filled with what had once been furniture: metal desks and chairs missing legs. I had no doubt that whatever was useful had long been carted away by Mighty's people and other scavengers.

The second room was empty of everything save a carpet of dust, in the midst of which was a perfect set of strange footprints that led to the far wall and then back again—they were short and broad, like a naked cat somehow deformed.

"Ransom! We must go soon!" Mighty called to me. I looked back to see him studying the ground.

I entered the third room.

It was shadowed, the windows blocked by more furniture that had been hastily assembled here—a desk on its side, bookcases . . .

Bookcases!

My heart raced for a moment, and I stepped my way over rubble to the partially visible furniture. In front of the two cases were piled chairs, and I pushed these aside until their pyramid crumbled and I was able to climb over what was left.

The left bookcase was bare, but the right one held two volumes in the lower shelf.

I strained to reach them.

Mighty's voice, suddenly close and sharp, hissed behind me. "Do not move, Ransom."

I froze with my hands on one of the books, and turned my head to see a pair of emerald eyes in a shadowed face staring intently at me.

I turned my head a few millimeters more and saw Mighty in my peripheral vision, frozen in place, his attention focused on the creature as he slowly removed something from within his robes.

He made a sign of silence, a finger to his lips.

The green eyes brightened, like two miniature green suns, and the thing leaped out of the shadows at me, hissing loudly. I saw long teeth and a broad snout and ears pressed back against its near-naked skull, and two gigantic paws full of saber-like claws flashing silver to either side.

Something hummed through the air, and the creature gave a startled cry of anguish and fell at my feet, its body tangling with a broken chair. It gave a rattling, long gasp of pain and then was silent.

"A wildcat," Mighty said, stepped to remove his weapon, a long, wide blade handled in what looked like polished junto wood, which I had never seen before, from the monster's neck. He wiped the blade on his robe and then replaced it in the folds within. He cocked his head sideways to study the beast. "Not a particularly agile-looking one, but he would have killed you."

I looked from the dead carcass, resembling a cat only in superficial ways—it was smaller, its pelt thinner, the head narrower. I had only seen pictures of them. They never stood on two legs, and long ago had been deemed animals by our scientists, a rogue turn in development.

"Thank you," I said.

He waved a hand in dismissal. "Come. We must go."

"In a moment."

I reached over the dead body of the beast to retrieve the two books. One of them, I saw to my disappointment, was only an empty binder, but the other was a real volume.

Mighty had stopped in the doorway, and turned to regard my treasure.

"Why do you go after such trifles?"

"It is not rubbish."

He started to speak, then held his tongue. "Come. We must ride back now before twilight comes."


**THAT NIGHT I STUDIED MY TREASURE IN MY TENT BY** lamplight. Myra and young Hera, intrigued by anything new, at first professed interest, but when they saw that each page was merely filled with scribblings much like the last, they grew bored and left me alone.

The language was similar to our own but difficult to understand. Other such books had been discovered, but they were very rare. From what I knew, the ones that had lasted were made of fine paper and preserved in dry climates. I knew in my heart that I held an artifact of the Old Ones in my hand.

I had hoped for pictures, but there were only a few diagrams and charts. The book's title, *Fuel Sources from the Martian Subsurface,* was meaningless to me, though I quickly gathered it had something to do with science.

An inscription in handwriting on the flyleaf was intriguing: "To Ben, Who Travels a Long Way for Love of a Planet, from Mother and Father."

Much of the rest consisted of discussions of how much of various elements, such as oxygen, was locked in the planet's soil, and how to remove it. The pages were very brittle, some of them flaking apart in my hands, so after a while I thought it best to put away my treasure, and did so.

That night, curling into my bed, I dreamed of an Old One named Ben, and of tall, clean spires and working machines, and plants nearly as tall, sprouting huge leaves showing the faces of ancients.

# ⊰ CHAPTER 7 ⊱

ANOTHER MONTH PASSED, AND MY BELLY GREW TO term. We had reached the central highlands, and the equatorial weather was warmer. There were pasturelands here among the dry plains, and no desert to speak of except in strange oases that sprouted like dusty pits in our path. The caravan had again doubled in size, and seemed more like a traveling circus than the ragtag army it was. I observed one raid on a convoy of L'aag tribesmen from the west traveling in steam motor vehicles; Mighty and his fifty or so soldiers, men and women, swooped down from our hill position and routed them within minutes. Not a gunshot was fired, not an arrow or blade used, and the convoy was soon on its way again, bereft of tribute.

Mighty came riding up the hill whooping like a schoolboy, carrying something long and colorful in his hand. He jumped from his horse beside where I lay nested on a bed of pillows, belly taut as a drum, and held it up triumphantly.

"A present for you, Ransom!"

He bowed and handed me the hat, a ridiculous thing of purple silk and a long yellow veil. I tried not to laugh.

"You don't like it? Then I will give it to one of my harem!"

He dropped it on the ground beside him as he sat down.

"So, Ransom, tell me, when will the kith be born?"

"Any day now," I answered. Feeling a pang in my belly I added, "perhaps any hour."

"And you are being tended to?"

"*Overly* tended to. Your harem bothers me by the hour with their attentions."

"You are not hungry?"

The thought made me gag. "No. Nor thirsty much, either."

"But you do drink?"

"Yes. A little." I thought of the bitter-tasting gemel tea, stronger and more bitter-tasting than usual, that young Hera had brought me an hour before, and had insisted I drink. I had not felt quite well since.

Suddenly the pains came very strong in my stomach, and I clutched myself and tried to breathe.

"I'm afraid—" I began.

And then blackness dropped down upon me.

## I AWOKE WITH TERRIBLE, DULL PAIN.

It was still daylight, though much later, by the height of the sun. I lay in my tent, on a mound of blood-stained pillows. Immediately I knew that something was not right.

Myra came in, carrying a bowl of water, and her eyes flared open to see me.

She dropped the water bowl and ran out.

"What—" I tried to say, but discovered I could barely speak.


I AWOKE AGAIN WITH MY HEAD CRADLED IN MYRA'S lap.

"Do not try to speak," she ordered gently.

"My kits—"

"They are gone," she said. "There were three—two male, one female."

"What—"

"Shh, do not speak. Mighty will speak with you later."

I looked up into her face. There was a strange, distant, faraway look in her eyes.

Suddenly overwhelmed, I tried to cry, but the pain was so intense that I could only go to blackness again.


A THIRD TIME AWAKE, THIS TIME NIGHT.

It was warm, and I felt a limpid breeze on my face. Myra was still there, curled on the ground beside me, asleep.

The breeze blew the tent flaps open, and I saw Mighty standing there, staring in at me, stone-faced.

"You've come to see me," I said.

He nodded, but would not enter the tent.

"What happened?" I asked.

"What happened is to my eternal shame. To think that I protected you these two months, only to let something happen right under my nose."

"What . . ."

"There have been many prayers, and a noon and two moon ceremonies." He turned away. "I hope someday to be forgiven."

He heard me try to speak and said in a pained, angry voice, "She *slept* with you under the same roof! *And to think she was part of my harem!*"

He beat his breast viciously with his fisted paw.

He lowered his head. "She has been dealt with. She was the daughter of my cousin Depal. The F'rar took him prisoner while we were in the south and threatened to behead him if she did not return to our caravan and try to kill you. She waited until you were to give kith, thinking you would be weaker. The gemel tea she gave you was laced with maroot. There was enough to kill two men. But the brunt of it went to the kits, who died as I watched them. Myra delivered them and I watched while they died cradled in her arms. *I cried!* They will be buried in the morning, if you will allow my ceremonies instead of your own. I am told it will be two days before you can rise."

He covered his eyes and wept. *"I am so ashamed."*

I could feel myself slipping back down into unconsciousness, but I managed to get out, "Don't be . . ."

He walked away without acknowledging my words, and then Myra was awake beside me, putting a wet cloth to my brow as I went back to blackness and dreams of dead children.

# ⇥ CHAPTER 8 ⇤

**MONTHS PASSED, AND WINTER WAS GONE.**

The moderate equator temperatures were beginning to flee, leaving a dry, blistering heat during the day and little relief at night. The caravan was packing, readying for the spring trip south and dispersal. In the end, after the various families of the clan had peeled off to their various ancestral homes, Mighty would be left with the small band of family and harem he had ruled when I first met him.

He had become distant in the preceding months, praying much, aloof at other times. His attitude toward me had not cooled, but it was as if a part of him, out of shame or honor or something else, had been shut off the day I lost my kits. In the beginning he stayed away out of respect, but after a while I felt there was something else, more deeply rooted, that kept him distant.

But I had not spent my time looking at the past. Each day I set aside a time for grief, and indulged myself. But I found that as the weeks went on, the time I needed became less and less. The kits I had never known would always hold a place in my heart, but it was as if that hollow hole were mending, leaving a tight, hard scar behind.

The rest of my time was well spent, also. I learned all I could about the ways of these nomads. Myra and I had grown as close as sisters, and I learned much about cooking from her and a fellow lately arrived named Hermes who, of all the clan, might be considered a chef. There were spices he used, gathered on his trips to the north, that were unknown even to Myra, and I watched with much amusement as she tried to glean these secrets from him with everything from flattery to threats of force. All the while Hermes would laugh, shaking his ample belly (he *did* like his own cooking) and waggling a claw-bitten finger at her.

"Never! Ne-*ver* will you find that out! Disguise yourself, Myra! Sneak up north like I did!" And then he would throw back his head and laugh as she hurled curses at him.

My body healed slowly, but well. In the end I became hard and strong, my face weathered and my muscles taut. I learned to ride much better, and I learned how to use weapons, and how to fight with my claws and my teeth if need be. I immersed myself in these things in the beginning to forget—but after a while, when my heart began to heal also, I found that I gained a new strength from them.

When Mighty and I did talk during dinner, it was not the same as before. I found that I missed these exchanges, and tried to reignite their fervor, but always he seemed to have his mind on other things. In the end I decided that we had become like a couple married too long. There was nothing left to say.

I didn't really believe this, of course.

**WE HAD OUR FIRST REAL DISCUSSION SINCE THE LOSS** of my kits on the evening before departure. The wagons were loaded, the horses weighted with booty and food-stuffs, the tents packed. We would sleep this night under the stars. The sun had just set, leaving a deep purple mantle across the west. It was a beautiful twilight. Overhead, Phobos moved like a slow, tiny beacon. Moon ceremonies were being held and, having seen them more times than I could imagine, and knowing that, in their huge circle, noses pressed to the dust, they would be praying for a safe journey, good fortune, and fine weather, I chose instead to study the horizon.

Mighty joined me without my knowing it. One moment I was alone, and then he was there, beside me.

"You left the moon circle early," I said, letting a teasing hint of scolding enter my voice.

"Yes," he said, seriously. "There are things we must discuss, Ransom."

In the darkness I turned to regard him. He was staring straight ahead, and his voice sounded strange—tense and almost nervous.

"What's wrong?" I asked.

He looked at me then, and I saw a look I had never seen before on his features—he was at a loss for words!

"If there's something you must tell me, hadn't you better start by opening your mouth?" I tried to be kind, but couldn't keep the teasing tone in check.

"Don't mock me!" he shouted.

Instantly I said, "I'm sorry," and for the first time since I had known him, I put my paw on his arm. "What's wrong?"

"You cannot come with us, Ransom. Unless . . ."

I waited for him to go on, but again he was tongue-tied.

"You're leaving me behind?"

"Anything but that!" he said. "This is very difficult for me . . ."

"Take your time," I said. "I'm listening."

He nodded. "Yes, that is very good. You always did listen, from the first time I saw you, smelling like bad red wine."

I smiled and he laughed. "I feel better now, and will ask you!"

He turned to face me, and something clutched in my heart.

"We have a way with our people—" he began, but I cut him off.

"You're going to ask me to join your harem!"

He stopped with his mouth open. "I—"

Flustered, I began to get up.

He took my arm, gently but firmly, and pulled me back down.

"Please listen to me before you speak!"

He was so upset that I complied.

"All right," I said.

He began again: "We have a way with our people. The clan leader, like me, has his harem when he is young and foolish. And then, as the old women say, he becomes even more foolish and falls in love. And this one becomes his queen, and the harem is disbanded forever. This is the way it is."

He stopped, but I said nothing, so he went on, now

looking directly at me. "When I found you, you were with another man's kith and I had no right of design on you. This was a matter of honor and law. When you lost your kith . . ."

He had continued to grip my arm, but now he let go. "It was a grave matter of lost honor when your kith was taken from you under my protection. Ordinarily I would have no right to approach you like this, but I have prayed to the sun for three months and the moons for two, and our shaman has said that I have atoned for my loss of honor and so might ask you to be my queen. I have noticed that you never spoke of whose kiths it was you bore, and I never sought to ask."

"It was my husband. He is dead, murdered by the F'rar."

"I see. But you never spoke of him."

I looked at the horizon, and tears began to form in my eyes. "That was because I did not love him."

I could feel his hope swell beside me, so I quickly went on: "But I loved his brother, and still do. My husband was the firstborn. It was a marriage of politics."

I turned to him with tears in my eyes and said, "I am so sorry."

There was still a strange look on his face. It was as if he had closed off one room and opened another. He nodded and said, "It is good that you tell me these things. It makes much clear. And it makes my decision clear, too."

He held up his hand before I could speak. "Please let me finish. I had my hopes, but they are not to be." He smiled. "I will be foolish with my harem for a bit longer, it seems. If you had consented to become my queen our path would have been strewn with rocks, but I would have cleared it for you. It would have meant danger for my clan but I would have endured it. Now that this is not to be, you must leave us in the morning. We will head south, to the Meridiani Pass, and you will head north with Hermes the fat cook, who will lead you to others of my brethren. They will keep you safe. There will be no repeats of what happened with Hera."

He looked at me, waiting for me to speak, and finally I said, "Why?"

"Because you are a great danger to us. The F'rar, and others, have been looking for you for months. Almost from the beginning I put whispers out, which eventually became shouts. I did not call you Ransom for nothing, Haydn of Argyre."

"So you know who I am."

"Tell me: were you named after that *composer* from the Jakra game?"

"Yes. My mother was a great lover of music. How long have you known?"

"From your third week with me. But those who would buy you back from me I do not trust. If I had handed you over to them you would have been dead by sunset of the day I did so. Nothing has changed. You have many enemies, it seems."

"Yes."

"And friends?"

"I don't know. I still don't know what happened that day the F'rar attacked my people down south."

He laughed bitterly. "What is it you don't understand? Your friends were beaten. The F'rar were there to kill you, and they failed. They will continue to try."

"Yes."

"That is why I send you north, where no one will know you. I release you from ransom. I would not have your blood on my hands."

"Thank you."

"Perhaps someday you will meet up with your people again, and put the F'rar in their place. I would send you to them now, but they stay well hidden, even from me. There is F'rar treachery everywhere these days. Apparently you are to be queen of a planet, instead of my queen. Your father, Augustus, never bothered us, and I trust you will do the same."

"I would be as good as my father to you."

"And if you had agreed to be my queen," he said, standing up and letting his paw brush my neck, "I would have fought armies from pole to pole for you."

I smiled up at him. "I believe you. And I will never forget you."

"Bah," he said. "After spending a week with fat Hermes, who never shuts up and never stops laughing, you will wish you had never met me."

"I doubt that."

"We shall see! In the meantime, sleep well, and I will take my leave of you before dawn. I will miss our talks, Haydn of Argyre. Even though I fear that this is best for both of us."

"I will miss our talks, too."

And then he was gone as quietly as he had appeared.

I sat a while longer staring at the western horizon, which had turned from purple to black.

I WAS AWAKENED AS THE SKY IN THE EAST BEGAN TO purple again with dawn. Myra shook me awake, and I rolled from my blankets and stood up to see a horse, a fine mare I had ridden many times, waiting for me nearby. My personal things, including my precious book, had already been tied in a bundle and secured to the mount. Straddling a second, larger beast was the cook, sound asleep in his saddle and snoring like a bellows.

I thought of what Mighty had said about spending a week with this man, and thought he might be right.

Mighty appeared just as the first jewel of sunlight split open the eastern line of the sky.

"The sun greets you!" Mighty said, slapping Hermes on the thigh.

The cook came awake with a snort loud enough to wake the rest of the camp, which, I saw, was already stirring.

The long caravan line of horses and carts was pointed south, while my mare, alone with Hermes's, was pointed north.

Mighty helped me up into my saddle and then turned back to Hermes.

"Remember everything I said, cook! If one whisker on her face is harmed I will boil you alive in one of your own soups!"

He blanched and began to blubber, but Mighty cut him off.

"Be quiet!" To me he said, "I would not send you with him if he was not the best tracker and bodyguard I have. You will be safe with him." He scowled at the cook. "Or else."

Hermes kicked his horse into a trot.

I made to follow, but Mighty held my reins. Myra, standing beside him, said, "Good-bye."

I bent down and kissed her cheek, and as I was straightening up, Mighty put his own lips on my own and kissed me hard.

"That is what you will be missing!" he said with a laugh, and then smacked the mare on the rump, making it jump and then settle into a trot, and I was away north, following the cook.

I looked back once, and Mighty had one arm around his harem girl, holding her close, and the other held aloft in his sign of peace, four fingers splayed from the thumb, claws retracted. At his feet was his dog Little One, panting.

I could not help it: tears welled in my eyes.

I raised my own paw in farewell and duplicated the sign.

Hermes, a few paces in front of me, already began to complain: "Catch up, will you! We've got to make Schiaparelli by noon ceremony!

I kicked my pony gently to urge it on and was soon astride the fat cook.

Without warning, he broke out into song:

> Oh! The traveling road's for me,
> A traveler's what I am,
> I hunt for spice,
> And play with the dice,
> And see what I can see!
>
> The road is ever wide
> And so am I you see!
> So if you meet up,
> Please do share a cup!
> The traveling road's for meeeeee!

He looked at me out of the corner of his eye and grinned. "You will find I cannot keep quiet," he said, and laughed, a basso rumble.

"So I've been told. Your voice is not bad."

He managed to bow while hardly moving a muscle.

"Thank you. My father and his father were singers. I thought of singing but found I loved to cook."

"Where are your people from?"

"Many of them are from Schiaparelli, which you will see later today. It is a small city but has enough troubles for a large one. It is an . . . interesting place. It is always my first stop on my spice tour. They serve an ale there that you will like."

"What if I were to tell you I don't like ale?"

"Everyone likes ale!"

"We shall see."

"You are a strange one. Mighty told me you love to talk back and make jokes."

"Only when jokes are appropriate."

"Ah."

He was silent for a few moments, but only a few. "Tell me what you think of my cooking."

"It was edible, what little of it I could keep down."

He boomed a laugh. "For breakfast I shall make you something that will make you *sing!*"


WE STOPPED WHEN THE SUN WAS A PAW'S WIDTH above the horizon, and he made good his word. His horse was packed all around with bundles and baskets, and they must have been in some sort of order because he went here and there among them, sometimes reaching an arm through one layer of packages to reach a parcel in the second layer. He was a magician with pot and fire, and soon had a tidy little flame going that gave off very little smoke.

"One of my secrets," he said, sprinkling a fine gray powder over the open flame, which immediately reduced its smoke almost to nothing.

"Something else you wouldn't share with Myra?" I teased.

"Bah. She was a charwoman at the stove. I am an artist!"

"We'll see."

And I did, for what he cooked for me was delicious, even though I could swear he removed it dry from a pouch and then softened it in water.

"What is this?" I asked, impressed and amazed.

"I will tell you what I tell anyone who asked—it is food!"

At the scowl on my face he added: " 'Food' is a precious word, my dear. Don't ever forget that. Without it what would we eat—dust?"

He roared a laugh and sank his teeth into some of his own creation, bringing his bowl to his lips and using neither utensil nor paw.

I used my paw in the fashion Mighty had taught me.

"Tell me more about the north," I asked.

He lifted his fat jowls from his bowl and looked at me in surprise. With one forearm he wiped his dripping lips. "That is like asking me to tell you about the whole world!"

"I am from the south, another world."

"Ah, then you know nothing about my land?"

"Only what I've read in books."

"As I said, then you know nothing."

He returned to his meal momentarily, then wiped his lips again. "It is a vast expanse of extremes," he said thoughtfully. "The winters are longer and harsher than in the south. The lakes often freeze, though never the Utopia Ocean, which is laden with salt. A good sea salt, when I can get it. It is colder at the cap than in the south, and there is more snow. Then come the highlands, which are rugged and for the most part lush. The city of Cassini is the grandest of cities in this part of the world. It is where I trade much of my spice. It is comparable to your southern city of Wells, only more—how do I say this—*rugged*." He grinned, and once more ate.

When he finished and dropped his bowl with a belch onto the ground, I asked, "What about the lesser cities?"

He became thoughtful. "There is Robinson, of course, but that is a strange place, full of outlaws. Then there is Sagan and Shklovskii, the twin cities, which in some ways are even stranger. They are near the lowlands and deserts. There are many outlaw scientists there, practicing strange arts."

"Such as?"

He waved a paw in dismissal. "Blasphemous things. Airships that will fly without balloons—as if the gods would not swat them down like flies! Mechanical motors that don't run on steam. Then after the highlands come the lowlands, which quickly become dunes and desert. The Baldies live there, of course."

His talk of flying ships intrigued me, but so did his mention of the Baldies.

"Tell me about the Baldies," I replied.

"What's to tell? You avoid them! They are like wildcats with intelligence! Which will not prevent them from eating your flesh! But at least they will discuss it with you in guttural terms while they are cooking you! We will avoid them, believe me. I know ways through the deserts"—he pointed to his laden horse—"I have maps and charts that took me years to acquire that will get us through any part of the lowlands. There are some interesting things there."

"Such as?" I told him of the place Mighty had shown me, where I found my precious book.

He nodded, without much interest. "Like that, and more. In fact, there is a place near the ruins of an ancient city that is exactly like what you describe, only much larger. It is on one of my maps. But we won't be going that way."

He saw the dejection on my face and added, "But we will see other things that will no doubt amaze you." He shrugged. "If you are interested in the past."

"And you aren't?"

"Me? I am interested in two things: shen"—he rubbed a finger and thumb together—"and spices. The two of them are often the same thing."

"And cooking?"

He pondered this. "Yes. But cooking without spice is nothing. It is boiling water and roasting dead things." He groaned himself to his feet. "But come. We must be on our way if we are to make Schiaparelli for noon services."

WE MADE SCHIAPARELLI AT TEN MINUTES TO NOON. The city appeared as a shimmer on the horizon, which soon resolved into a wide, dusty blur and then, abruptly, an oasis of sound and drab color. It seemed to be one vast market stall. We passed under the watchful eye of a sentry in a low tower guarding a gate in the low, rugged stone wall surrounding the place. He seemed more interested in what Hermes had in his hand and tossed to him as we rode by than in ourselves. Hermes never broke stride or looked at the scraggly fellow, but a slight nod passed between them after the sentry caught and checked the coin in his paw, and that was the last we saw of him as he retreated into his tower.

I had become so unused to masses of people that at first

I was uneasy. Hermes must have sensed this because he turned to me and shouted above the roar of the milling crowds in the dusty streets, "It is different from Mighty's camp, eh?"

I nodded, and he laughed.

"Don't worry, my dear. I have two men to see, and then we will be off on the road again."

I noted the decrepit clock tower in the middle of the square, a copy in miniature of the one on the imperial tower in Wells—its hands were just reaching noon.

"What about services?" I shouted.

He laughed. "That is just something I tell myself to make sure I'm on time for other things!"

No one else seemed to be slowing down as the rusty-sounding chimes gave off the hour of the day.

We drove our mounts as best we could through the milling throng. I saw cats in various strange garb—tall, stiff hats, scarves composed of acres of colored silks, one fellow who seemed to be dressed like a metal man, in armor. Among them I saw the distinctive red tunic and watchful, suspicious eye of the F'rar guard. My heart skipped a beat.

But my companion rode oblivious through all this, a pleasant, expectant grin on his countenance, so I tried to follow suit.

No one seemed to have the slightest interest in us until we came to one of the few prosperous-looking structures in the town—a two-story edifice of red brick with gold-painted cherubs with wings and paws stretched toward the sky, full-sized statues mounted to either side of the gold-painted door. The door was half open, and a tall, thin, sharp-eyed, and prosperous-looking gentleman stood with his arms folded, smiling hugely.

"Hermes!" he shouted as we dismounted and tied our mounts to the post to the left of the door. The man came all the way out and greeted my companion with a hug. He then abruptly pushed the fat cook away and stood regarding me with wary interest.

"And who is this?"

"My cousin," Hermes said. "That is all you need to know, Dardo."

Dardo let his eye linger on me for one more moment before turning back to the cook. "So tell me! What have you brought? My chef is dying for more takka root!"

"I have takka root coming out of my ears!" Hermes said with a laugh. "And I have no doubt that your cook uses too much of it!"

They both laughed, and Dardo pushed the door to his establishment wide and bade us in.

I entered into gloom suffused with eye-hurting beams of light streaming in through tall windows. The room was cavernous, with a long, dark bar along one end to the left, and a huge dining area overlit by those windows on the right. Ceiling fans turned lazily below the lushly painted ceiling—there were scenes of ancient battles and love scenes immediately identifiable from various ancient poems and myths. I noticed that the scenes began chaste over the dining area near the windows and grew increasingly less so until, as they reached the bar, they became downright raunchy.

Hermes threw his arm around my shoulder and drew me toward the bar. "Come with me! You'll get a neck cramp looking at that junk. I have *ale* for you to try!"

I sat with him, and Dardo himself served us from behind the bar.

I stared at the drink before me: a huge, tapered glass,

dark brown as a toasted nut, and frothing foam on the top as if Olympus Mons had come back to life.

"What is—"

"That, dear cousin, is Volcano Ale!" He pointed to Dardo, who gave a slight nod of his head. "That highway robber behind the bar brews it himself in the cellar!"

They both waited for me to taste it, and I did so, cringing until the first sip produced a wonderful explosion of sweet berry and fruit tastes on my palate.

I must have shown my pleasure because they both laughed.

Hermes grinned at me from ear to ear. "What did I tell you about ale! But be careful—this stuff is stronger than it tastes!"

He turned to Dardo, and the two of them began to discuss business as if I weren't there. The ale kept me company. When the first was finished a second magically appeared, and it was somewhere in the midst of this second helping of pleasure that I noticed the tiring effects it was having on me, which did not keep me from finishing a third when it was put before me.

I found myself leaning against Hermes, my eyes half closed.

"What? Is little cousin so tired? Perhaps she should take a nap." He laughed. "I told her it was strong and she didn't believe me!"

I nodded vaguely and, vaguely still, noted that the fat cook was now helping me up a wide, beautifully carpeted stairway, with Dardo leading the way. The innkeeper held a large ring of jangling keys in his hand, and selected one as he went along.

"In here," I heard him say, and noted that we had stopped before a particular door of rich, dark wood. There was a cameo of a female cat's face, the princess from the legend *Ailla,* laid on its surface.

I heard the key rattle in the door, felt myself move forward, saw a rectangle of shaded window and then felt the cool, soft hands of a pillowed bed, something I hadn't slept in in months, enfold me like the arms of a mother.

And then I heard myself gently snoring, then heard no more.

Until Hermes came back to kill me.

I CAME INSTANTLY AWAKE. I DID NOT KNOW HOW long I had slept, but I heard the door to the room ease open and felt as much as saw the figure standing over me, holding a long blade.

"Poor girl," Hermes said. He sounded very drunk. This was confirmed a moment later when he leaned over me as I feigned sleep and I smelled the thick odor of Volcano Ale on his breath. My paw went to my belt under the folds of my robe and stayed there.

He stood swaying with the long blade in his paw and continued to look down at me.

Suddenly he staggered back a step and collapsed to the floor, weeping.

"I am not a murderer," he said with a sob. "Of all the things I have done, I cannot do that!"

Stealthily, I brought my own blade out and slipped out of the bed behind Hermes, pressing the blade to his throat.

"Why were you going to kill me?" I whispered. "Tell me or I will cut you."

He gasped and dropped his own blade, which I kicked into the corner.

*"Tell me!"* I ordered. "Or I'll bring you back to Mighty myself and let him deal with you."

This brought on a fresh bout of weeping. "It's no use, Ransom. By now Mighty is gone. *They're all gone!*"

I pressed the blade deeper into his throat, and a chill went down my spine. "What do you mean?" I asked with a hiss.

"They're dead by now. The Meridiani Pass, they were to be waylaid there."

I nearly cut him, such was my rage. "How could you do this!"

"How could I *not*?" he wailed. "The F'rar have taken my entire family hostage in the east! Just as it was with the girl Hera." He looked up at me with haunted eyes. "They drew and quartered my brother Timon! They cut out my father's tongue—and he a singer! And said they would do worse to the rest of them if I did not do as they asked and delivered you to them. If they had known you were still with Mighty you would be dead by now. Because I did not trust them, I told them you left a week ago and that I was to meet you on the way north. But still they insisted on attacking Mighty, to make sure. We were lucky to leave when we did."

"Mighty trusted you!" I responded.

"It is the worst thing I could ever do!" He buried his face in his paws and wept. *"But they have my family!"*

"What were you to do after you killed me?" I asked him.

Still weeping, he said, "Bring your body to them as proof. Then they will let my family go."

"They won't, and you are a fool. I suggest you go to the morgue and find a suitable replacement for me."

He looked at me in horror. "The F'rar will kill me!"

"If you follow me, or ever come within my sight again, fat cook, I'll kill you myself," I said. "I am sorry for your family, but what you did cannot be forgiven."

He looked up at me with a kind of pleading in his eyes. "Mighty never understood that the world is changing. It is a different place now than it was only a few months ago. The F'rar have changed everything. . . ."

"And this is what you do to a man who loved and trusted you?"

"These F'rar are not bound by honor! *I had no choice!*"

"There is always a choice. Good-bye, Hermes. If you had told Mighty, he would have knocked down heaven to free your family. Instead you betrayed him."

I left him there, weeping.

I expected that the door might be watched, but this was not the case. There was a back stairway that led to a storage room and a door into an alley, and, as luck was with me, I was able to mount Hermes's laden but stronger horse, leaving my poor mare for the traitor, without being seen. I made sure to transfer my things to the larger animal, including my precious book.

After riding slowly through the market square and under the unwatchful eye of the tower sentry, whose snores could be heard from the ground, I kicked the horse into a full gallop, already afraid at what I would find at the other end of my short journey.

# -⊰ CHAPTER 9 ⊱-

**NO ONE WAS LEFT ALIVE.**

They had been caught in the middle of the Meridiani Pass, just as the fat cook had promised. I wished at that moment that I had slit his throat. From a distance the bodies looked like a string of beads laid out between the wagons, which had been undamaged. Mighty had not even had time to draw the caravan into a circle. I soon found out why: the F'rar had taken a page from Mighty's own book and hidden themselves in ground traps. A line of these crossed the path of the front of the caravan, and Mighty's body lay here, punctured by many bullets and arrows. Myra's body lay next to him, similarly violated. The rest had been attacked from the sides and from above. Little One had died at the feet of his master.

It must have been over very quickly, and signs of the

overwhelming force the F'rar had brought on the little caravan were evident. The rest of the dogs also had been slain.

As the sun lowered itself, I cradled Mighty's head and said some of his own prayers, trusting that his gods would forgive me for using noon ceremony ablations at evening.

I then buried his body with Myra beside him, and tended to the burial of the others as best I could.

It was a long night, and I spent it toiling by the light of Phobos, which kept me company in my labors. I recited one of the moon ceremony prayers as I worked:

> *O mighty son of the sky,*
> *Fierce night warrior,*
> *Guardian of the dark ways,*
> *Help me in my pursuits*
> *If they be worthy ones,*
> *And let me not stray*
> *From the path of righteousness,*
> *From the road of good deeds,*
> *And from the way that leads*
> *To the well-being of my people.*

I had tears in my eyes as the sun rose, and I mounted my laden horse, turned my back on the circle of graves, and left that place.

# PART TWO

# SCIENCE

# ⊰ CHAPTER 10 ⊱

AT FIRST I HAD SOUGHT TO TRAVEL SOUTH, TO LOOK
for Kerl and the remains of my people. But the way was
blocked at every turn. There was a massive F'rar presence
near the equator, and the news was that what had been my
people, who were now called rebels, had been scattered to
the four winds and were being systematically hunted. I
concluded that even if I reached the spot where I had last
seen them, would they be anywhere nearby after these
many months? The best thing seemed to be to find my way
safely to one of the smaller cities in the north and try to fer-
ret out the resistance from there.

Hermes's maps were as good as he had claimed, and I
had no trouble getting to my goal. And, somehow, the fat
cook had done his job well. When I rode into the city of
Shklovskii three weeks later there was, to my surprise,
much F'rar presence, and much commotion among the

populace. But none of it was over me, because I soon discovered that I had been declared dead and was therefore no
longer a threat.

The F'rar had moved on to other things.

I was dead, which in many ways was a good thing.

SHKLOVSKII WAS NOT MUCH OF A CITY, AND NEITHER
was its twin, Sagan, but I soon learned that, as with any
place, there were layers to the onion that could be peeled
away, revealing more beneath than was apparent on the
surface. My bedouin garb immediately attracted attention,
not all of it good, and I was nearly detained at the city gates
until I produced a packet of takkra root, a bribe that gained
me instant admission.

"So you are a spice trader?" the guard, suddenly civil,
asked.

I nodded.

"Then you will be staying at the House of the Fox?"

"Of course," I answered, having no idea what he was
talking about.

He lowered his voice. "You might not find it as con-
genial as in the past. There are"—and here he lowered his
voice even more, forcing me to bend my head toward
him—"F'rar in residence. You might find the *Eagle* to be
more to your liking." He straightened. "Even though my
brother-in-law runs it, and is a dolt, it is better than the *Fox*
these days. And the ale is superb."

"Volcano Ale?" I asked, failing to keep the sarcasm
from my voice.

He spat. "Swill from the midlands. I wouldn't wash my
horse's arse with it."

I smiled, thanked him, and handed over another packet of spice.

He bowed. "Is there anything else I can help you with?" He looked me up and down. "The best places to eat? New places of business?" He studied me again. "Consorts?"

I employed his advice on the first two and went on my way. For a brief moment I thought of soliciting his thoughts on the rebels, but was sure that information would quickly find its way to unhealthy places for me.

I did follow his advice and avoided the *Fox*. The *Eagle* was a rodent hole, but a serviceable one. Its very disrepute had kept the F'rar away. After paying the innkeeper extra to watch my horse and its wares, and warning him in a civil way (which I'm sure he was used to) that if anything untoward happened to either of them I would cut his throat, I ventured into the sunlight to get my bearings.

It wasn't long before I saw a column of red-shirted F'rar leading a feline down the street. The citizenry made a wide path and avoided the eyes of the fellow, who knew some of them by name and shouted to them for support, which was not forthcoming.

When this episode was over I asked a citizen standing next to me, who had looked away as this went on, what it meant.

"Are you kidding? They will never see him again. No doubt the F'rar wanted his business, so they took it. It is the same all over." He stopped to study me more closely but I quickly said, "I have been on the road a long time."

"Well, if you're a trader, hide your wares, because sooner or later the F'rar will confiscate them."

I bowed in thanks, and ate a meal in one of the places recommended to me. I avoided the ale, which was just as well, because the food was worthy of a trough, the atmosphere uncongenial. Also, I continued to draw attention because of my garb.

When I returned to the Eagle I found the innkeeper rifling through my horse's bundles. Stealthily, I drew my blade and lay it against the back of his neck.

He jumped nearly a foot, and fell to the ground stammering his innocence.

I told him to get up.

"What were you looking for?" I asked.

"It was . . . apparent to me that you carried more than just spices. There are men in Sagan who would pay dearly for some of these materials."

Though I had no idea what he was talking about, I encouraged him to continue talking.

Still cowering, he reached toward one bundle, and then another. "These chemicals, for instance . . ."

"Yes?"

"It's just that, as I said . . ."

"Point me toward these men. They are not friends of the F'rar, are they?"

*"No!"* Realizing that he had spoken too quickly and with too much enthusiasm, he lowered his voice.

"Come have a drink with me and I'll tell you more."

"I think not." I hefted my blade. "We'll talk here. What's your name?"

"Pavin."

"Talk then, Pavin."

He told me of a place in Sagan in which I would find a fellow who would lead me to another place, and so on. When he was finished I asked, keeping my voice level, "Are these men of the rebellion?"

His eyes widened with sudden fear. "I know nothing about that! Nothing!"

I paid him in spice, offering more if he stayed away from my belongings, the edge of my blade for certain if he did not. I was learning that most people listen to you if you offer to end their lives if they do not.

It was late in the day now, and I had one more task before the shops closed. There was a milliner down two streets and over one, and after asking advice of passersby, determined that it was the best in the area. I entered, and exited half an hour later dressed more in line with the local population and carrying my robes in a parcel under my arm. It felt strange to be wearing cultivated things again— a skirt, blouse with leather jerkin, some costume jewelry— and at first I felt awkward and out of place. But soon I noticed that I was drawing attention no longer, and became at ease.

I returned to the *Eagle* and inspected my room, which was nearly absent of light, smelled dank, and sported nothing worse than a peephole, which I covered. Then I went out again. It was already dark, and streetlamps were lit, something else I hadn't seen in a long while.

I had another wretched meal, drawing some attention now not for my dress but for the fact that I was female (this bar, it turned out, served mostly workingmen), and then went back to my poor room and slept.

Or rather tried to sleep, because my dreams were bad ones, filled with all of the treachery and death I had recently seen.

For the first time in a long time I felt very alone.

It was not a feeling that would last long.

# ⇥ CHAPTER 11 ⇤

I WAS AWAKENED BY LOUD KNOCKING ON THE DOOR.
It was late. A single shaft of light beamed through the tiny
window onto the floor. I had meant to get up at dawn.

The banging continued and I yelled, churlishly, "Leave
off that! I'll be there in a minute!"

A sudden thought struck me that it might be the F'rar—
but this was instantly dispelled by the certainty that they
never would have knocked except to knock down the door
itself.

"Who is it?" I shouted.

"It's me! Pavin! The innkeeper!"

Hearing that, I lay curled back into the surely tick-
ridden bedding. "Leave me be! I'll be down presently!"

"Then you'll surely lose your chance, miss! I'm detain-
ing him as it is!"

"Who?"

"Someone you should meet! He's in the taproom!"

I heard him recede and I called out, "All right! I'll be right down!"

"Very well!" his fading voice answered, and then I heard his boots on the stairs.

I reached for my bedouin robe automatically, and then spied the neatly folded pile of city clothes on the room's single chair and pulled them on instead, groaning as I did so. What little sleep I had attained had been bad. The bed was too soft and the room too dank. And now I had to wear these horrible clothes again and forgo the comfort of my robes.

I NONETHELESS MADE MYSELF PRESENTABLE, AND five minutes later entered the taproom.

It was empty—but not quite. In the darkest corner behind the end of the bar was a table. The single occupant, in dark clothing and a cap, had his back to me and the room.

Pavin appeared at my elbow and urged me on.

"He's paid his bill and is about to leave!"

"Bring me some breakfast—and it had better be eatable," I ordered.

He was studying my new clothing, about to make comment, but I ignored him and walked to the table, crossing to the opposite side and pulling a chair out.

I sat.

The stranger raised his eyes from his steaming cup. I could smell strong coffee.

For a moment I thought he wore a mask, but saw with a start that it was a trick of the bad light—his face was smooth, nearly devoid of fur, the eyes deep blue and piercing. He was no doubt a member of the L'aag clan, known for these features.

"I hear you are a person of interest," he said. His voice was low, gravelly, tinged with irony.

"It depends on who is interested."

He gave a low snort and waved a paw—again nearly devoid of fur. "Is there anyone in this town except the F'rar who aren't aware of you?"

"Did Pavin contact you?" I asked.

"Not exactly. Let's just say that we become interested when any spice trader enters either of the twin cities."

"You wish to talk?"

He leaned his head closer to mine. His eyes were nearly blazing, and his lips pulled back in a smirk.

"I wish to know, first of all, how someone like you ends up with Hermes the fat cook's wares."

The eyes didn't blink, and the grin widened.

"So . . ."

"Yes," he said, leaning back. He sipped his coffee without taking his eyes from me. "I was told you arrived in bedouin robes. Were you his . . . apprentice?"

"Something like that."

"It doesn't matter," he said. "When Hermes was executed by the F'rar, we feared his particular talents were lost to us. But perhaps not."

I realized that he was trying to hide his jubilation.

"Then we will deal," I said.

"Oh, certainly." He barked a command to Pavin, who appeared instantly.

"The lady is checking out of your pisshole," he said without taking his eyes from me. "Gather her things."

"Of course!"

"And Pavin," the stranger said, "I will inventory her

horse very carefully. If anything is missing I will do twice to you what she would have."

"Yes! Yes!" the innkeeper said, scuttling off.

"He would have been subtle, but things would have been stolen."

"I caught him at it yesterday."

He laughed, and pushed his chair back and rose. He was easily the tallest feline I had ever seen.

"We must go by back ways," he said, which did not surprise me.


WHEN WE HAD LEFT THE CONFINES OF SHKLOVSKII, by a wayward route I could never repeat even if I could remember it, there was time for more talk. But my companion, curiously, had become almost uncommunicative. At first he grunted at my questions, and then ignored them. We were on what looked to be a little-used road, roughly paralleling a main thoroughfare a good half kilo to our left. I could see knots of travelers passing both ways there, and an occasional flash of a red shirt, which explained our slow progress through this trail of muck and gullies. In the distance, growing ever taller, was the silhouette of another town with the same basic outlines as the one we had abandoned.

"Answer me something," my riding companion said, long after I had given up any hope of discourse.

"Yes?"

"Would you hesitate to kill Frane, the leader of the F'rar, if she stood before you now?"

Without thought I said, "No."

He nodded. "And tell me this. Would you hesitate to do

the same to the so-called queen in whose name the rebels fight?"

I went cold. "But she is dead."

He raised an eyebrow. "Is she? It is rumored that your late companion was charged with killing her, and did not do the job. The F'rar produced a body, but I happen to know it was not who they said it was. The real body was never found. In any case, the rebels still fight in her name, even though the F'rar claim she is in the afterlife."

"I know nothing of this."

His eyebrow was raised again. "Is that so? Do you mean to tell me you traveled with Hermes, yet knew nothing of his charge?"

"Hermes was a traitor to his people. *My* people."

"Ah." He reined his horse around to face me. We had stopped in a stretch of woods, thin white hinto trees whose pale pink leaves waved lazily in the faint breath of wind. I had already reached for my blade and held it in my right paw, against my side. My companion bore no weapon that I could discern, but I had no reason to believe his intentions were good.

"Perhaps the time for talking has passed," I said, fingering the blade nervously.

He looked surprised. "Oh? I had gathered it has just started. I just want to know where we stand."

"We stand nowhere. I will take my spices and leave."

He gave a graveled laugh. "That is the only thing I cannot let you do. We will trade mounts, if it comes to that, and you will ride off unmolested. But your spices, especially the more . . . exotic ones, must go with me."

"You mean the chemicals?"

He raised an eyebrow. "Yes."

"Who are you?"

"I am called Newton."

The name meant nothing to me, and he seemed surprised that I did not know who he was.

"You do not know of Newton of Sagan?"

"I'm afraid not."

His entire manner seemed to relax. His smile softened. "That is a good thing. Then perhaps you are who you say you are."

"Yes, perhaps."

"How did you come by these spices, then?"

"Hermes laid a trap for my people, with the F'rar, in Meridiani Pass. I got away and hunted him. Then I stole his mount."

"You didn't kill him yourself?"

"I had my chance. But I knew the F'rar would do it for me."

"By the way, what are you called? The registry at Pavin's foul hole called you 'Ransom.'"

"That will do."

He nudged his horse around and rode on, pacing me. He was silent again. We broke out of the little copse of trees and into a wilder expanse of sand and mire, with few bushes between ourselves and the main road. He didn't seem concerned.

Suddenly he drew up short and reined his horse to the right. I followed, though I could see no reason. The ground looked the same—broken and marshy.

"You didn't see the quicksand?" he asked me.

I shook my head.

"Well, we've now determined that you've never been this far north before."

"True."

Again he was silent, and I watched the city of Sagan

rise before me. The road to our left drifted off that way toward a distant gate. Our own progress led us wide of the town, flanking it.

From here the city looked exactly like its twin: dark, decrepit, with low buildings and a half-guarded wall.

We soon came to a break in the wall surrounded by debris. My companion ignored it and we rode on.

"It's not much farther," he explained, without so much as turning to look at me.

We passed more rubble, some of it curious, on the outskirts of the city. I saw a field of huge rusted tubes, and another of strange, abandoned machinery—boxes and gargantuan spools of cables and a veritable mountain of delicate-looking glass cylinders of various colors, collecting dust under the gloomy sky.

"One of our storage areas," Newton said cryptically. "What is the phrase? Best hid in plain sight."

I could not imagine what use anyone would have for this field of junk.

So abruptly that I almost ran my horse into his, Newton turned into a hole in the wall. Not a hole so much as a cut, with a low ceiling of crumbling brick that caused me to lower my head almost to my saddle. The wall was thick, nearly two meters, and as I passed through, I heard Newton chuckle in front of me.

"Don't fear—those bricks over your head were assembled to look dangerous. They're as solid as the rest of the wall. F'rar and others unfriendly to us don't like to poke their noses into openings like that."

I came out the other side and found my host waiting for me. We were in a tunnel little wider than the wall opening. It would be impossible to get two horses abreast here, and a raiding party would have to enter one man at a time.

As we went on at a slow canter, Newton called back, pointing overhead: "You will notice the slits at the top of the wall. Unwelcome visitors would be met with a nasty surprise."

There were openings that looked like darkened windows along the corridor, and I asked Newton about them.

"We are being watched," he said simply.

After a quarter of an hour, the narrow tunnel suddenly ended. I saw that a long, narrow pit extended in front of Newton's horse. He waited patiently, and now I heard a rumble, which became insistent.

A platform rose into place, and the pit disappeared, leaving a smooth metal floor that conveyed us to a door.

"Beyond this door you become a member in standing of the Science Guild. Hermes was such. You will not have full rights, but you will know enough about us that you would be a danger to us. If you agree to enter, you also agree that there is only one way to leave the guild."

"Feet first?" I quipped.

Newton smiled. "I will use that phrase in the future. I was going to say by old age. Soler will enjoy your wit."

He studied me closely. "Do you agree?"

I nodded. "I agree."

"Very well."

Without Newton's insistence, the door opened with a clang, and we were led into a cavernous room filled with more noise than I had ever heard in my life.

# ⇥ CHAPTER 12 ⇤

THAT I WAS WELCOMED WITH GRAND CEREMONY
would be an understatement. Or, at least, my horse was. A
gaggle of faces and many hands reached for us with excited voices as we entered the room, calling the horse by
name (which I did not know), Standard, stroking his muzzle, feeding him oats, and stripping him bare of every
package, parcel, and bundle. Only my private effects in the
saddlebag remained. In minutes I stood feeling naked, my
mount showing himself to be the ugly packhorse he was,
now contentedly munching on a bag of grain that had been
secured to his muzzle. The packages were carried off with
triumphant cries of "Ooooh" and "Ahhh!" but one figure
stayed behind to study me.

Newton, who had sat on his own mount through all this
with an amused look, bowed slightly toward the figure and
then toward me.

"Soler, meet Ransom. Ransom, Soler."

"So pleased to meet you!" Soler said in a high, almost wheezing voice. She sounded genuinely pleased. A pair of spectacles hung around her neck on a piece of twine, and she absently drew them up onto her nose, squinting at me through them. She was stout and broad-faced, with a long mane brushed back away from her pinched features.

She reached a sudden paw up and shook my own.

"Welcome!" she said.

"Ransom has been informed of her status," Newton reported.

"Excellent! Are you hungry? Do you require a meal?"

"We ate at the Eagle, in Shklovskii," I said.

She laughed, almost a cackle, and the glasses dropped back down around her neck. She turned and clapped her hands. "Then you definitely require a meal! Luther!"

A short, dark cat appeared, hunched over, almost walking on all fours. He had a dour disposition.

"Make a luncheon for our guest and for Newton. Come to think of it, I'll join them also. I haven't eaten since—"

"Since your last meal forty minutes ago," Luther said in a desultory way. He turned, shaking his head, and slouched off.

"We shall dine in my office!" Soler announced, and we moved off through a sea of milling workers split into teams. The cavernous floor of the complex was roped off, literally, into what seemed to be work areas. Each had one or more benches and tables covered with bizarre instruments or machines. A spray of sparks went into the air at a distant table, and there was a groan followed by a hoot of pleasure. The place was unbearably noisy.

As we made our way through this madness I looked up: the ceiling was crisscrossed with catwalks and electric lamps. There were duct openings, and a thin line of windows at the very top of each wall. Somewhere a generator hummed.

With a start, I realized that some of this equipment was very similar to what I had seen in the ruins Mighty had taken me to.

"We're underground?" I said out loud.

"Of course!" Soler shouted above the din. "Only way to keep things hidden!"

Suddenly the noise went down and then almost disappeared as Soler ushered us into a dark, stuffy little room and slammed the door behind us. The space was cluttered with boxes and shelving and papers—and books of the Old Ones on a bottom shelf beneath two crammed shelves of more petite, smaller feline volumes.

There was an entire row of them, ten at least, with bindings of different colors, behind the desk where Soler now sat. She told Newton and me to sit also, and as there were no chairs, I followed Newton's lead and cleared a crate of piles of papers and used it to sit.

Almost immediately the door opened, letting in noise and Luther, who bore a tray as if it would break his back.

He complained constantly as he served us, then was gone, leaving a last insult behind him. The door banged shut behind him with finality.

"You enjoy soup?" Soler asked me, putting her spectacles back to her nose to study me.

"Of course. Though I have been used to dog stew."

"Dog!" she cried in alarm and dropped her glasses. "How barbaric!"

"Our guest was living with the equatorial bedouins," Newton explained. "Though I venture she was not born to them."

I held my head up proudly. "Too much culture for a Yern?" I asked.

"No. More the way you took to city clothing when you abandoned your robes. As if you had been quite used to them in another life."

"Perhaps."

"Perhaps you'll tell me about it."

Under Newton's intense blue eyes I answered, "Perhaps."

"Now!" Soler interjected. "Let me begin by thanking you for bringing us Hermes's chemicals! We had quite given up hope of ever seeing them. When he was . . . when he met his unfortunate . . . when . . ." She looked at Newton for help.

"When he was killed by the F'rar, we thought our work would have to stop. But now that you've taken on his routes . . ." Newton smiled.

"I didn't say that," I replied.

"I know. It was mere hope on my part. Is there any chance?"

"Frankly I wouldn't know where to begin."

Soler's countenance darkened. "Oh, dear. So this means that what we have now will be the last that we see?"

Newton turned to her. "I am working on other avenues. They will not be as convenient as Hermes was, though."

"And you're sure he did not give us up?"

"I think we would have heard from the F'rar by now if he had. But my ears are still to the ground."

"Good. Good." Soler bent to her soup again, using her wide spoon to slurp it into her mouth, until she stopped suddenly with a pained look on her face and turned her head sideways to squint at me.

"You did say *dog?*"

"Yes. It was quite tasty."

She shivered and went back to her meal, shaking her head and saying, "barbarian" between mouthfuls.

"May I ask you about your books?" I ventured, after trying the soup myself. It was bland enough, with overcooked vegetables, a hint of leeks.

At first there was no response, but then Soler had finished her soup, tilting the bowl up to her mouth with her paws.

When I repeated the request she blinked at me and said, "Yes?"

I pointed to the shelf behind his head. "Your books."

"Yes, of course! You like their colors?"

"Excuse me?"

She swiveled in her chair and plucked a volume from the shelf. It was blue all around, with a blank cover.

My heart sank, and continued to sink as she opened the book to show blank pages.

"Are the rest just like this?"

"Of course! We call them 'notebooks of the Old Ones.'"

I noticed that Newton was regarding me quietly with his blue eyes and ironic mouth.

"I have something that might interest you," I said, and got up. I felt Newton's gaze following me as I left the office, made my way through the labyrinth of noise and commotion (I watched two young assistants bent intently over a silver box that suddenly spurted flame, driving them back with cries), and went to Standard, my horse. I retrieved my treasure from his saddlebag and returned to the office (passing the same two young assistants, their faces covered with soot, once more studying the same singed box, if anything from even closer quarters now), shutting the door behind me. When I regained my seat I saw that Soler was studying my half-full soup mug with barely concealed interest.

"This will make you forget soup," I said, handing her the hefty volume.

For a moment she looked at it with indifference, studying its bland brown cover, but then her eyes widened as she opened it at random and saw columns of figures.

"Oh! Oh!" she cried, overcome with excitement. She rifled through the pages and held it up for Newton's examination. "Look!"

"I've already seen it," Newton said wryly.

"I figured as much," I said to him.

"The innkeeper Pavin was going to make off with it, but I convinced him otherwise. I was waiting to see if you would do the right thing."

"The right thing?"

His wry smile widened a millimeter.

"Or you would have confiscated it," I stated.

"Of course."

Soler was lost in her enthusiasm, giving little bleets of happy disbelief. "Where did you get this?" she asked.

Newton seconded the question, and I told them of the facility Mighty had taken me to.

"An oxygenation station," Newton said with certainty. "We must mount an expedition if possible and see if there is anything else of use there."

Soler nodded absently. "Naturally . . ."

Newton said to me, "Much of the facility you are in now was outfitted with equipment from a similar station twenty kilometers from here. It was in very bad condition, but we saved what we could. There is another station near Robinson, and rumors of others in the south. At one time, long ago, we believe they produced oxygen and pumped it into the air."

"Why?" I asked.

"Because it was needed," he replied. "Some of our people believe that at one time Mars had a very different atmosphere. It is one of the questions we are trying to answer here."

Soler held the book up again, pointing with a trembling finger to a particular page. "I'm not sure, Newton," she said, her whiskers trembling with excitement, "I'm not sure, of course, but this book might provide us with . . ."

"It might at that," Newton answered cryptically, but when I looked to him for explanation, he said nothing.

Soler looked at me. "Thank you, Ransom! Thank you!"

She half rose, tumbling the book to the floor, and after retrieving it with a startled cry and laying it gently on the table, she reached out and took both of my paws in her own.

"You have done us a great service," she whispered, her eyes filling with tears.

"We should go," Newton said, as Soler nodded and sat down, opening the book at random and immediately losing herself in it.

"You can have my soup, too," I said as I rose. Soler mumbled thanks, not hearing a word I said, as she ran a bitten-to-the-nub claw over one page and then another.

"YOU DON'T REALIZE HOW HAPPY YOU'VE MADE her," Newton said outside, raising his voice to be heard above the din.

"What did she mean when she said that volume might provide you with something?"

Newton shrugged. "We're working on many things here, Ransom. Perhaps I'll tell you another time."

"Perhaps," I said wryly.

He smiled thinly and led me on. "There are things I must attend to," he said. "But I'll leave you in good hands."

We stopped at a table where nothing seemed to be happening. There was an anatomical chart on a stand, and in a chair a slender fellow with a long, thin face who was so deep in his own thoughts that he didn't even acknowledge our existence.

"Is he blind?" I asked.

"On the contrary," Newton replied, clapping his paws in front of the fellow's face.

The other made a startled sound and then looked at Newton as if trying to focus on him. Suddenly he did and leaped out of his chair to take the other cat's arm.

"Newton! So happy to see you!"

"I have someone I want you to meet, Jeffrey," Newton said, and introduced us.

Jeffrey took my arm and said exuberantly, "Hello!"

Newton pulled up a second chair, and told me to sit in it while he spoke to Jeffrey in private for a moment. Then Newton turned his attention back to me.

"I will find you later. We will dine together. As we speak, some of Hermes's spices—the real ones—are no doubt making our bland soup taste better."

He took his leave, and I was faced with Jeffrey, who once again had sunk so deeply into his own thoughts that he seemed in a trance.

"Jeffrey?" I said tentatively.

He suddenly began to speak, staring straight through me. "Did you know," he lectured, "that at one time a cat was no larger than half a meter in length?" He held his paws apart that distance, and without waiting for me to comment on this startling disclosure, he went on. "We have fossil records of this. In fact, at one time millennia ago, cats were smaller on average than your common house dog, and had tails. The brain of this ancient cat, we deduce, was not much more developed than a dog's. But over time, this changed. There are fossils of these intermediate-growth steps. Some of them are *startling*."

He rifled through the charts and papers on his desk, putting before me a set of drawings depicting the fossilized remains of various carcasses. They were numbered, and as the numbers increased, the bodies showed distinct differences. The legs of the early samples were like that of many four-legged animals, designed to that mode of walking. But then the legs began to elongate, the thighs slim, becoming narrower and the pelvis turning upright while the chest grew wider and the arms and fingers longer, slimmer, elbows less pronounced, the tail vestigial. It was a remarkable transformation.

"This happened over millions of years, of course. Now we use our paws with dexterity, and only walk on all fours when at extreme rest. In another hundred thousand years I imagine the pelvis will straighten to the point that even this facility will be gone."

"And you're the first one to study this?"

He blinked, and said in wonder, "I really don't know. It certainly is fascinating, though, isn't it?" He pointed to the various drawings laid out before us now in a row. "This was from the Tharsis region, and this one I unearthed near Chryse Ocean . . . and this one at the steppes of Arsia Mons. Did you know," he said, abruptly changing his tone and topic, "that some of these developments were dead ends? As if nature were tinkering, trying to find just the right brew! The modern-day Baldy is a descendant of one of these false steps of nature, with his near-naked carcass, smaller stature, and tail. As much animal as feline. So is the wildcat, even more so. I call this science developmentalism. Over such vast stretches of time . . ."

He went on like this for what seemed like hours. Though I must admit that much of it was fascinating, I found myself eventually settling into a kind of stupor.

Occasionally he asked me a simple question, and I caught him studying my features closely at one point.

"Hmm?"

"I'm afraid—" I began.

Suddenly Newton was back.

"So, Jeffrey," he asked the developmentalist, "what do you deduce?"

Jeffrey instantly turned his attention from me to Newton. "She is definitely from the south, with a ninety percent probability that she is from the city of Wells. Perhaps born to the west, in Argyre. The speech patterns, shape of the skull, the mannerisms all point to it."

"Only ninety percent?" Newton asked.

Jeffrey blinked, his long, serious face missing the joking tone of the remark. "I'm sorry—isn't that enough?"

Newton threw back his head and laughed, his voice low and rasping. "Quite enough, Jeffrey. Any chance she was reared by a bedouin clan?"

Jeffrey blinked. "Oh, no. Absolutely none."

Newton put a paw on Jeffrey's arm. "Thank you, my friend."

Newton led me away, and said, "So, Ransom. Did you find Jeffrey's theories . . . interesting?"

"Are you happy with yourself for tricking me?"

"Not at all. I know as much now as I did before I gave you to our developmentalist. We shall leave it at that for the moment."

We had reached one wall of the amphitheater, and a door opened for us into a dark corridor.

"Come with me. There's something I want to show you," he said.

I followed. When the door behind us closed the sudden lack of noise was palpable. There were dark windows in this corridor, and as we passed these windows Newton gave a lazy wave.

"Acknowledging your spies?" I asked.

"Those spies are what keep us from destruction." He stopped and looked at me seriously. "I don't think you realize how important we are."

He didn't wait for my reply but walked on.

When we came to the end of the tunnel, a solid rock wall, there was another window in the sidewall, and Newton turned to it. "Out, please," he said.

The wall dissolved, and there was an open doorway to the darkness beyond.

"How did you—" I said in wonder.

"We do many things here," he said quietly, and stepped outside. "It was actually an illusion of sorts."

It was a cool evening, and the smell of outside air was refreshing. We were in a small grotto, nicely sculpted gardens with a platform in the center. It was surrounded by red brick walls on all sides.

"This is lovely," I said.

"Yes. Please, follow me."

He led me through the path toward the platform. On either side were beautifully tended plants. In the tepid light of Deimos overhead I saw that each was labeled. Many were fragrant flowers, and the air was rich with their perfume.

The platform was up a step, and Newton held his paw out to help me. I refused it. Even in the scant light I could see him smile.

Something was mounted in the middle of the platform on a pedestal: a white tube pointing toward the heavens . . .

"A *telescope!*" I marveled.

"You've seen one before?" he asked.

I was going to say that, yes, I had, in the royal tower, but held my tongue.

"I've heard of them," I said instead.

"Hmm, yes."

He bent over the lower end of the tube, and looked in for a moment. I tried to hide my excitement and impatience.

Finally he straightened and said, "Please look."

I bent, seeking the ocular with my eye. For a moment I saw nothing, then moved my eye slightly, and there was a blue-green marble swimming in a sea of space.

"Earth!" I gasped.

"Yes."

I took my eye away from the telescope and studied the area of the sky where it pointed.

There, sure enough, was the planet Mighty had called the Blue Lady.

I studied the planet through the instrument again: a mottled place suffused with yellow-white clouds, a few dark land markings, polar caps and the overriding blue that gave it its predominant color and name.

"The blue is water, we're fairly sure of it," Newton stated.

"But so much of it! It can't be!"

"Because Mars is so shy of it?" he responded. "It is true our oceans are shallow, and our riverbeds sometimes dry. Why can't Earth have more water than Mars?"

I stood away from the instrument. "Why have you shown me this?"

He hesitated, then shrugged in the near dark. "Let me show you something else."

He pointed to another part of the sky, where the Great Shawl, a gauzy white immensity of, I knew from my studies, billions of stars, stretched like a baby's blanket across the sky.

"Are you going to tell me that it really is a shawl?" I joked.

I thought I heard him chuckle. "What if I were to tell you that each of those stars may have planets around it, just as our own Sol has Earth and Mars and the others?"

I said nothing.

"This is something else we study here. Along with biology, and the fossil record, and the workings of machines like the one that projected that natural-looking wall at the end of the tunnel we just came through. We now have a land machine much more efficient and reliable than the steam-powered ones you've seen. And many, many other things."

I felt his passion as he continued. "These are immensely important things, Ransom. Important for this planet and for our people. We must be allowed to continue this work. If the F'rar were to find and destroy us, it would be a tragedy immeasurably beyond our own mortal destruction. It could mean the end of life on Mars."

"What do you mean?" I asked.

"We believe that the atmosphere is slowly losing oxy-

gen," he said. Again, his way of simply stating what was
on his mind managed to startle me.

"How do you know this?"

"We have instruments, we have done experiments, we
are in the process of building—secretly, of course—a research station atop Olympus Mons. There have been rudi-
mentary balloon flights, but the F'rar either shoot them
down, thinking them enemy reconnaissance, or sometimes
they fail. But yes, Mars is losing its atmosphere."

"How long . . .?"

He shrugged. "We're not sure at this point. But let me
ask you: wouldn't you want to know?"

"Of course."

He nodded, satisfied at my answer. "Come with me."

I followed him off the platform (once again refusing his
paw; his was an old fashioned gesture) and through the
garden to what seemed a back wall but proved to be an en-
trance to a house. We mounted three stone steps and stood
before a common red wooden door, which he opened with
a key. Inside was a foyer, and a well-lit and cozy living
area bordered by a smaller room. The other side of the living area—which, I noted with joy, contained a compact
upright *tambon*, an instrument in which, alas, I was badly
talented—opened out into a grand dining room flanked by
a neat and tidy kitchen. The table was set for two places,
and candles were lit.

He smiled. "I told you I would offer you a good meal."

We sat while menials of some sort—not servants, he
later explained, but rather apprentices in the guild—appeared and served. The meal was excellent, and there was
an exquisite wine.

He talked through the entire meal. I answered his questions politely, but there continued a wariness on his part, as

if he were circling me, trying to decide when and where to strike.

Finally I asked him, "Do you have much news here of the rebels?"

"Ah," he said. "I thought you might find interest in that. Mostly through spies, though we do have a crude radiographic system that works occasionally. The trouble is finding someone reliable on the other end to talk to. But yes, we do get news, as it comes. Apparently the F'rar are having some trouble crushing the entire planet."

I nodded.

"You are pleased with this?"

"Why wouldn't I be?"

"Talking like this could get you executed these days."

"I suppose. But does anyone dare not feel this way, at least in their hearts?"

"You must understand something," Newton said as the plates were cleared away and a dessert wine, along with a frozen concoction that tasted like lemon-flavored ice shavings, was served. "These are very devious times."

"I well understand that."

Remembering Hera and Hermes I thought, *More than most*.

"People," he continued, "will do what they must to continue with what they love and see as important. Sometimes men wear two masks."

He was staring off into the distance. I was puzzled by this remark, but let it go.

He rose, and put his napkin on the table. "I would like to show you something else," he said.

I followed him across the living room, with its carved wooden chairs covered in dark fabrics, its low lamps, its warm fireplace kicking sparks and filling the room with wavering, dancing light, its precious musical instrument, to a smaller room beyond. It was a kind of study. It also was richly appointed: a huge carved desk of junto wood, a tall chair behind it, and the desk facing a wall composed of another, smaller fireplace and rows of shelves above it.

He took something down from a shelf and handed it to me. Remembering what had happened in Soler's office earlier, my heart did not leap at the sight of this book, until I saw that its cover was graced by an inset picture.

"Open it," Newton offered.

I did so, and a riot of color leaped out at my eyes. It was *filled* with pictures of the Old Ones!

He took it gently from my hands and turned to a specific page. "It is a picture book of great minds of the ancients."

I continued to stare as he stopped at a particular portrait of an Old One, looking as always naked and wrinkly, the features sharp and almost frightening compared to our feline ones.

Under the picture was: SIR ISAAC NEWTON.

"It was after him I named myself, years ago. I was not given his name at birth. As far as I know I am the only feline ever to bear his name.

"Who was he?"

"A great scientist of the Old Ones." He closed the book and returned it to its shelf. "Unfortunately, my picture book contains little more than pictures. It may even have been intended for a child of the Old Ones."

"So—" he began, but at that moment a doorbell rang at the other end of the house, and he held his thought, waiting. In another moment one of the guild's apprentices, looking nervous, appeared in the doorway to the office and announced, "It is Carson, sir."

"Show him in," Newton said. To me he said, "It's best if you stay here, and out of sight."

I saw why, a moment later, as Newton, suddenly stiff, slipped from the office, closing the door all but a crack behind him, and marched forward, paw extended in greeting, to a red-shirted commander who was just entering the living room.

"Carson! So good to see you!" Newton enthused.

The other took his paw briefly, unsmiling, but settled himself without being offered into the most comfortable chair in front of the fire. Newton took the lesser chair beside him. An apprentice appeared with a tray. Soon the two felines were smoking and studying glasses of what looked by its familiar bottle to be brandy.

They talked, and I tried to listen, but the red shirt's tones were low, and Newton spent much time nodding. When one of the apprentices appeared behind them unannounced, Carson spun on him and shouted, "Get out, you rodent! How dare you!"

The boy nearly ran from the room, and the conversation continued in even lower tones.

The fire was low when the red-shirted commander stood and stretched. The brandy bottle was nearly empty. Most of it, I noted, had gone into Carson's gullet. He staggered slightly on getting up, laughed and this time shook Newton's paw vigorously.

"A good evening! We will do this again soon!"

"Of course!" Newton rejoined, with less enthusiasm. "Anytime!"

The red shirt took a staggering step forward, and knocked something, which broke, from a low table. Ignoring the damage, Carson stumbled on, making it to the front hallway and then disappearing. There was another crash, and then Carson was heard shouting, "Out of my way, you dolt!" before finally the front door was opened and slammed shut, and he was gone.

Two of the apprentices, looking haggard, appeared in the doorway to the living room, and Newton dismissed them. He knelt to examine the broken shards of what had been on the table, lifted them gently, and held them to the light for a moment before placing them, just as gently, on the table from which they had been disturbed.

He walked thoughtfully toward me as I opened the door.

"Did you hear any of it?" he asked.

"Very little."

He nodded, and opened his paw. A tiny sliver of broken blue glass lay there.

"It was a present from my daughter," he said wistfully. Then he bade me come back with him to the living room, and after fussing with the cushions, made me sit in the comfortable chair the red shirt had vacated.

I sat, and immediately felt a sharp, thin stab in my posterior; the pain immediately receded when I shifted my weight. I thought I had sat on another sliver of broken blue glass.

He emptied the brandy bottle into a new glass for me, and then stirred the fire into last life. For a few moments we sat in silence and watched embers spark and settle, and listened to their sighing rustle.

"So you see," he said at last, "that a man can wear many hats."

"You're a collaborator?"

"Hardly, Ransom."

"What do you do for that creature Carson?"

"As a scion of the oldest family in Sagan, it is my duty

to safeguard its citizens." He turned and gave me a tired smile. It was then that I realized that he was older than he looked. "I'm helping the F'rar to track down the Science Guild, which is rumored to be very active in this part of Mars."

"Carson is a fool."

"Thank the One for that. And pray Carson continues to be one. Because of my station, my grounds and my garden have not been searched. I am accorded this luxury. I will do everything I can to continue in that fashion."

He breathed deeply. "I am very tired, Ransom. It has been a long day. I have arranged, if you are willing, for you to sleep in my spare room. It is off the hall to the right. Either that or you can find your way back through the garden and sleep with the other guild members."

"Thank you, I will stay. It is very kind of you."

He nodded. "The bed will suit your bedouin ways?"

I returned a ghost of his wry smile. "I can always sleep on the floor."

"Sleep well, nevertheless, Ransom."

"Thank you."

I got up as he did, and made my way to the hallway. I turned right, and saw two closed doors, one on either side of the hall. I walked back to the living room to ask him which door was meant for me.

I stopped dead in the opening, and observed Newton kneeling over the chair I had just vacated. He was searching the cushion carefully for something, and then drew something up and into the bare light of the fire. It was needle thin and silver. He examined it for a moment, and then nodded and placed it in a small, long box, which he closed with a click.

Then he rose.

I retreated into the hallway, checked the door on the left, which proved to be a bath, and then quickly entered the room on the right. I closed the door softly behind me and turned on the light, which was electric. The room was bathed in faint light.

It was a girl's room. The walls were a muted blue shade, tacked with lace at the corners. The bed was small, lovingly carved, the headboard pictured with kits at play with two smiling moons overhead, as if guarding them. A delicate coverlet, cream-colored, looked handmade.

There was a tiny table next to the bed, with a photo in a light blue frame. It was of a young woman of about my age standing beside the railing of a bridge and smiling. Behind her was a vast empty space, with a canyon wall in the hazy distance and a pale pink sky overhead. She looked very happy.

I turned out the light, climbed into the bed, and was asleep almost instantly.

Sometime during the night I started awake. From somewhere deep in the house came a single long moan of despair, and then silence.

For the rest of the night there were no more sounds.

# ⊰ CHAPTER 13 ⊱

MY TIME IN SAGAN FLEW BY. SPRING WAS ALREADY
turning to summer. The days grew hot and dry. While not
a prisoner, I yet felt myself under guard constantly. When
not in Newton's company, which I often was, I was always
given an escort, who usually proved to be more minder
than source of enlightenment.

An exception was the geologist Merlin who, while in
many ways as odd as the rest of the scientists I had met,
was in other ways the least so. She had an ardent interest
in areas outside her own, including, to my delight, music
and dance. The trouble was, while talking with her about
one of these disciplines, she might without warning return
to a problem she had been having in her own work. A conversation about ballet might suddenly become one about
aquifers.

I learned that there were certain areas of the under-

ground facility that were off-limits to me. One day while
in Merlin's company we wandered unobtrusively into one
of the many tunnels that led from the main building. This
one, I instantly noticed, was different. The walls and floor
were of smooth metal, and the slope indicated that it led
farther underground than the main facility. There were no
dark windows in the walls save at the beginning and at the
end, which we reached after a very long walk. It was here
that we were confronted by a lone, startled guard and a
wide-open door that led into a second facility nearly as
wide, but not nearly as busy, as the one above. Before the
guard blocked my view I saw a long structure, a sleek
black shape supported from below in many places and that
dwarfed everything around it.

"How did you get down here?" the guard, dressed in a
brown uniform cinched at the waist with a bright gold belt,
shouted. Behind him the door was already sliding closed.

Merlin, taken out of her reverie, merely stared at the
guard and then looked around us with confusion. "I have
no idea."

Already, more guards appeared behind us, and we were
escorted politely but forcefully back to where we had entered.

I noted that when the door closed, there was no indication that there was a tunnel there.

I continued to sleep in Newton's guest room and to take
meals with him. That night at dinner, I waited for Newton
to mention the incident, but he said nothing of it. Overcome with curiosity, I brought it up myself, but he merely
waved a hand and said, "We do many things here. Not all
of them are as evident as others."

That very night I was awakened again by a single moan
from somewhere in the house. This time I rose and tried to

find its origin, but I was unable, due to the brevity of the sound, to locate it.

I did discover that night that the doors to the house were locked against entry.

And, of course, exit.

ONE EVENING, PERHAPS THREE WEEKS INTO MY TIME in Sagan, Newton proposed at dinner that I accompany an expedition mounted by Merlin to a geologic site not far away.

"It's a good time for it, and perhaps the only chance we will get for some time," Newton explained. "The F'rar army in this area has retreated for the moment. The word from my people on the ground is that it is safe to do outside work." He paused. "Since you are interested in F'rar progress, I'll tell you that we've heard from some of our southern friends, and that things are very bad there for the rebels. We can expect, I would think, more refugees from the south, as well as more F'rar after them.

"I should also mention that if things work out, there will be another expedition in a few weeks, to one of the oxygenation stations to the east. I would like you to accompany me on that."

"Of course."

"Since you've already visited one, you might find it of value."

I agreed.

"Good, then."

"How do we get out of Sagan without being detected?"

He smiled. "Carson is coming for drinks again tonight. I will make sure one of his patrols to the northwest is pulled south to look for rebels."

• • •

THAT IS EXACTLY WHAT HE DID, AND THE NEXT DAY
Merlin and I, along with two apprentices, left Sagan unac-
costed to the north. I was not surprised to see that Jeffrey
also accompanied us, since it was his practice to tag along
with any expedition, to hunt fossils.

It was not much of a trip, since we traveled in a motor-
driven vehicle. This was nothing like Mighty's caravan. It
was noisy and barely more comfortable than a horse cart.
Including the driver, we sat two abreast in three rows inside the boxy structure, with windows open to the dusty
air. There was a road of sorts, but it was not well paved,
and we bounced along as if we were a kit's toy marbles
shaken in a can.

"Wouldn't it have been faster to ride horses?" I ventured, raising my voice to be heard over the jouncing, and
the complaining screech of the contraption's motor.

"Faster, yes, but not practical," Jeffrey said with a
frown.

Merlin elaborated, indicating a fourth, empty row of
seats in the rear: "For specimens!"

I was going to propose a horse-drawn cart, but my
words were drowned by a particularly jarring creak of the
vehicle, and the fact that Jeffrey and Merlin were continuing a running argument they had had since we left Sagan
about the best topsoil indicative of some mineral or other
beneath.

So I contented myself with the scenery for a while:
rolling valleys spotted with sandy patches and grassy
knolls, the occasional stand of junto trees, and something
that winked in the distance like a strip of silver. I thought
it was an optical illusion, a mirage, but as we drew ever

closer, it only grew and lengthened and hurt the eyes more with its brilliance.

"Is that water?" I asked, but my two companions were locked in their argument and unavailable for comment.

Half an hour later we had drawn up beside the shore of what was unmistakably a lake, one of the largest I had ever seen. Blue-green water, cloudy with sediment, gently lapped the silty beach, and I could just make out the far shoreline, nearly lost in a self-made haze.

"What is this?" I asked.

"What is *what?*" Merlin responded, standing beside me and studying the water intently. "Did you see a lake creature? If so, Jeffrey would be ecstatic. One of his goals is to capture a live specimen. The only fossilized remains he has are in horrible shape."

I pointed at the water itself.

"What is this lake called?"

The diminutive cat immediately lost interest. "Oh. Lake Cassini. One of the Crater Lakes. They feed most of our aquifers, the best until you hit the pole. A good source of drinking water after filtering. The others are bigger, but Newton thought it safer to go only this far. Besides, we still have good work to finish here from the last expedition. . . ."

She said this as she was walking away from me, and by the time she had finished, I doubt she even remembered that she had been talking to another person.

In minutes the two scientists had established separate camps, and each was banging away with hammers and other instruments at old, established sites.

I found a soft dune and sat contemplating the lake for a bit. There were only a few times when I had been this close to large bodies of water. In my mind they were always associated with enchantment. One of the few memories I had of my mother was of a lake trip outside Wells when I was just months old. She was still trying to recover from my birth and that of my brother, who was stillborn. The gloom in the palace had been palpable, and when someone suggested that my father take my mother to Lake Christy, he had assented. The ride out, in a royal carriage, had been quiet, but when we topped a short hill and the lake—little more than a craterlet filled with upsurging water that was dry as a bone half the year but that swelled to overflowing in the spring—came into view, there was an audible gasp from my mother. Then, as if the sun had come out from behind a cloud, she smiled. It was the only time I ever saw her smile.

But her delight now was palpable. Before the carriage had even stopped (which caused my father some alarm), she scooped me up into her arms and was out the door and running to the water's edge. She kicked off her slippers and waded in, and forever will I remember the look on her face as she held me before her. It was suffused with pleasure, yet there were tears in her eyes.

"Look at the water, Haydn!" she cried, and then she swung me down so my naked feet just touched the water. It felt like warm velvet on my toes. She did it again, and now I was laughing along with her.

Later we sat on the perfect beach, and ate a picnic lunch that had been packed with care and now was unpacked by my mother with abandon. My father later told me that it was the last time he saw her eat a hearty meal, and the last time she was happy. She died weeks later, still weak from the birth complications and beset with fever. I was not at her bedside when she passed, but my father said that her last words, in the feverish glow just before death, when she up in bed and stared at unseen things, were "Look at the water, Haydn!"

I found that there were tears in my eyes, but they abruptly dried at the sight of something moving across the lake toward us like a shot. It was a craft of some sort, low and wide, which glinted like a coin on the sparking surface of the water.

The two apprentices had already seen it also. One of them was now armed. The other roused Jeffrey from his pit. The paleontologist came reluctantly, slapping dirt from his paws, to stand and regard the newcomer.

"Oh, drat," he said, "it's him."

The armed apprentice raised his weapon, but Jeffrey put a paw on his arm to stay him as the craft drew near and then, with a sudden turn sideways, beached expertly in front of us.

It was a boat, as smooth on top as the sides, with a pointed bow and a tiny, windowless cabin. It looked to be made of wood, but with a polish that was nearly gleaming. It was painted all in bright blue, to blend with the water.

The cabin was not windowless after all, but, I noted, inset was the same sort of one-way mirror employed in the tunnels of the Science Guild.

We waited. Then there was a sound like a *pop* and the top of the cabin flew back on hinges and up rose a face suffused in a massive yawn.

"There already?" the creature said with bare interest, stretching his paws out and then shaking himself awake as he climbed out of the cabin and stood on the smooth deck. He was handsome in a roughish way, dressed in short breeches and a red undershirt. He studied me intently while speaking to Jeffrey.

"'Lo, Jeff! Thought maybe we could do a littl' tra-ding. Who's the girlie?"

It was the oddest accent I had ever heard—a mixture of extreme northern stretched vowels with the tinny edges of the east.

Jeffrey looked first at Merlin, who had emerged from her own hole and stood absently dusting herself, and then at me.

"Girlie?" Jeffrey asked.

The boater laughed, then jumped into the water and waded to shore. "Never mind, my friend. Saw you tro' my scope and thought I'd take a row over and see what's to be!"

He was still studying me intently—as a wife on a budget might examine a fish at the market. I turned to Jeffrey and said, not hiding the scorn in my voice, "Who *is* this creature?"

Absently, Jeffrey said, "That's Pelltier. Lives in a camp on the other side of the lake. He buys and sells things. He's useful at getting us parts and such now and then."

Pelltier would not stop eyeing me, and now gave an elaborate bow. "Would love to show you my place sometime, girlie. Fit for a queen it is!"

Merlin scoffed: "Ha! It's a shanty town! Smells like oil and old beer!"

Pelltier cocked an eyebrow, still bowing. "Nevertheless."

Jeffrey intervened, "I'm sorry, Pelltier, but we have nothing to trade today. On a bit of a light expedition." As if a sudden thought came to him, he added, "You don't happen to have anything in my line, do you?"

Pelltier stroked his chin. "I mi' at dat. Be gla' to let you 'ave it on credit, long as payment was for 'coming."

I could see Jeffrey struggling with this proposal. "Credit? We've never dealt like that before."

"No, we 'ave not. But this is a very special piece, yes? Per'aps a down payment?"

He was still looking at me.

"I don't understand you," Jeffrey replied. "And besides, this isn't the way to do business—"

"While you was diggin' your beans out'n the ground here, I did a little excavatin' of my own on the other side of the lake. Pulled a skel'tin of one of them old fellers out'n the ground."

Jeffrey's eyes went wide. "An *Old One?*"

Pelltier nodded. "More'n likely. Ugly as sin he is." He was still looking at me, and his smile widened. "In'trested now, Jeff?"

"I should say so! Let's see it!"

Pelltier hooked a thumb behind him. "At my camp. If you and the girlie would like to come wi' me . . ."

Jeffrey was confused. "Merlin or Ransom, here? Why can't you and I—"

"Ransom, as you call her." He finally addressed Jeffrey directly, and his manner was all business. "A twenty-minute trip in my boat, Jeff, and you get to see sometin' you've been lookin' for your whole life. What say?" His smile was back.

Jeffrey looked at Merlin, who shrugged. "I'll carry on here," she said.

"Better yet," Pelltier offered, "why don't ol' Merlin here take your motorcar 'round the lake and meet us there later? This ways, if you likes what you sees, you can haul it back for keeps!"

Jeffrey suddenly smiled. "Of course!" he said.

• • •

TEN MINUTES LATER THE THREE OF US WERE CRAMMED into the very strange cabin of Pelltier's noisy boat, which, he informed me, ran on a steam engine he built himself from parts traded with the Science Guild. As he worked the controls, Pelltier made sure to keep crowding against me.

"Don't get many girlies in these parts," he whispered at one point, grinning into my face. Up close he smelled of garlic and tobacco.

"Do you by any chance have cigarettes?" I asked.

"I should say so!" he said, and reached into his tunic, pulling out a pack and giving one to me.

I put the precious cigarette in my pocket to save.

The lake was choppier in the middle, but only Jeffrey seemed affected. He tried to keep his eyes on the horizon, but I saw he was having difficulty. By the time we neared the far shore, he was beginning to swoon.

"Hang on, Jeffrey," I said to him, putting a paw on his arm. "It won't be long."

He nodded and closed his eyes.

"Not quite, girlie," Pelltier said suddenly, turning the wheel sharply to the right and making Jeffrey groan. I saw out of the one-way glass something long and dark rise in front of us, like an impossibly long eel. In five minutes we had circled out of its way and were back on course. Pelltier returned to his placid demeanor.

"What was *that*?" I asked.

"They don't like to be disturbed, girlie. Riles 'em up and they sends up a tentacle or two. Prob'ly bothered his sleep, we did. But we're okay like fish now. Back on course and all. Almost there!"

And then there. I couldn't believe the city of tents camped on this far shore. They were brightly colored like a circus, red and blue and yellow. Some even sported pennants at their tops, flapping in the breeze. I counted at least twenty.

We pulled into a jetty made of solid wood. I counted three other boats of varying sizes, from dingy to small freighter. Someone in short breeches was there to meet and help tie us down. There were others milling about in similar outfits.

"What is this place?" I asked.

"Pelltier City, of course!" he answered, throwing the hatch up and clambering out. He reached a paw down to help me up.

"I'm fine," I said.

"Suit yourself," he said with a shrug, and jumped away.

I helped the still-swooning Jeffrey up the recessed ladder and over the top to the deck and then the dock. It was indeed like a small city, with activity everywhere. A small harbor crane was being moved into position to load a pallet of goods into the belly of the freighter. Its smokestack gave it away as a steamer, the first I had ever seen outside of pictures in books.

Pelltier was talking to a small group of men just off the dock, but when we approached he told them "Get to it" and turned his smile again on us. "Follow, Jeff!" he ordered, and then took us through the maze of tents, each of which was open for business, each stocked to the tent poles with goods in open crates and boxes. One green tent held fresh produce, another housewares, another tobacco (how my mouth watered!) and liquor and other vice goods. Pelltier had a sudden thought and stopped here, spoke to the woman in charge, and then took something from an open crate. He then turned, grinning, and tossed it to me.

"Catch, girlie!"

It was a rack of cigarette packs.

"Finest Hellas tobacco!"

"Thank—" I began.

He laughed, waving off my thanks, and led us on.

Jeffrey had recovered at this point, and I could feel his anticipation grow.

"Pelltier, are you sure—"

"Oh, this one'll cost you, Jeff, and a pretty bit of change, too."

We walked beyond the last tent and kept walking, Jeffrey running ahead to catch up to Pelltier now.

The two of them went over a small rise and then down the slope, and when I caught up with them they were already in a wide pit. Jeffrey stood with his eyes wide.

"The trick," Pelltier was explaining, "was to move off the shoreline. I thinks to myself, if they was here, wouldn't they move back a bit from the edge of the water? More comfortable like. So I 'ad my boys dig around, and soon they comes up with Mr. Ugly 'ere. Actually, we calls 'im Rex, just as a joke, you see."

I climbed down into the pit and stood next to them.

"It's marvelous!" Jeffrey exclaimed.

Pelltier laughed. "Not a good bargaining tactic, friend. Your price jus' went up twen'y percen'!"

It was the skeleton of . . . something. It was long and partially twisted along its length, as if it had died in agony. It was similar to a feline skeleton but definitely not feline. For one thing it was a bit taller, and the skull was more elongated, the teeth blunter. The paws were not pawlike, the fingerbones longer and ending not in claw retractors but just ending. I had a hard time imagining what that paw looked like in life. The feet were similar, the anklebones more angular. It was a very strange specimen.

"I must have it!" Jeffrey enthused.

Pelltier slapped him on the back. "That's what I was counting on, ol' Jeff! We can start da price wi' girlie, here!"

*"What?"*

"The missy! Ransom! We can start by t'rowing 'er into the bargain!"

"That's out of the question!"

Pelltier's face darkened. "Why?"

I said, "Because I don't belong to anyone."

Pelltier looked at me closely. "I bet you don't at dat." He stared at me for a few more seconds and then sighed. "All ri' then. Worth a try, it was."

From then on he totally ignored me, and he and Jeffrey got down to serious negotiations.

By the time Merlin arrived with the truck two hours later, the fossilized remains of Rex were ready to be loaded into the bed. Pelltier begged us to stay for a meal, but Jeffrey, excited by his acquisition, wanted to get it home.

As we were getting ready to leave, Pelltier came up to me and bowed.

"Beggin' your pardon, ma'am, but you would 'ave made a fine girlie."

"I'm sure," I said coolly. "Is there anything you wouldn't buy and sell?"

"Not that I can think of." He laughed.

"How do you keep the F'rar from bothering you?"

He laughed even harder. "Oh, dey tried," he said. "Dey tried, and good. But dey found in the end dat it was easier to deal with us den bother us."

"So you give them what they need and want."

His laughter died as if a switch had been thrown. "I wouldn't exactly say that, ma'am." He bowed, and went to make final arrangements with Jeffrey.

•   •   •

ON THE RIDE BACK I ASKED JEFFREY WHAT HE HAD
given Pelltier in exchange for Rex.

He considered a moment, and then said, "Some scientific equipment and other goods. The usual."

"Aren't you afraid the technology you give him will
end up in the hands of the F'rar?"

Jeffrey blinked. "I hardly think so. Pelltier is one of the
fiercest rebel fighters in these parts."

I considered this, and felt better about the rack of cigarettes I held in my hands. I reached into my tunic, brought
out the single cigarette Pelltier had given me, and lit it.

"By the way," I asked Merlin, after I had lit the cigarette
and felt the first hot, acrid bite of tobacco I had tasted in
months, "do you know what Pelltier meant by calling me a
'girlie'?"

Merlin frowned in thought, then said, "I don't know
much about the customs of these pirates. I did pass a tent
filled with women of questionable employ, though."

"Yes," I said. "I passed that tent."

Jeffrey looked confused, so Merlin explained.

"What!" Jeffrey cried in astonishment, stopping the
truck (though I noted gently, so as not to disturb his treasure in the back). "You mean he wanted to buy Ransom
here for . . . ?"

"Could be!" Merlin answered evenly, and winked at
me.

As Jeffrey, blubbering outrage, started the truck up
again and drove on, I looked out the window, and smoked,
and said nothing.

# ⇥ CHAPTER 14 ⇤

MORE WEEKS WENT BY. THE HIGH HEAT OF THE SUM-
mer came and, just as quickly, passed. I fell into a routine
of sorts: up at dawn, breakfast with Newton, a few hours
of apprenticeship with Merlin or Jeffrey, and then the afternoons to sit in Newton's garden reading one of his
books or, if the spirit took me, a few minutes of bad music-
making on the upright *tambon* in Newton's living room. I
made what I thought were discreet inquiries as to what
went on in the chamber below that Merlin and I had stumbled onto that day, but found that most of the others were
not even aware of it, or at least cared not to acknowledge
its existence. The door never appeared again while I
watched.

One day while waiting for Newton to appear for dinner I
drew down from a shelf in his study the picture book he had
shown me that first night. It was a warm afternoon, the last

of the hot days, and too uncomfortable to sit in the garden. The pink sandstone of the house provided a cooler reprieve, and I decided to stay in the study and read.

I opened the book at random, trying to match the skeletal outline of Rex in my mind to that of the pictures I saw. Unfortunately, most of them were not standing figures but busts or head and shoulders only—and then I flipped the pages, and the book opened to a particular page and I caught my breath.

The caption under the figure said: FRANZ JOSEPH HAYDN.

And under that: *Composer.*

It was a full figure of an Old One with a mane of white hair and a chiseled, somehow noble look on his ugly, nearly naked face. His eyes looked kindly, though, and in his long frame I could almost superimpose the bones that Jeffrey had purchased from Pelltier.

This, then, was the true origin of my name!

My mother, who had been so in love with music, must have known. I flipped through the book looking for other composers and found two: a funny-haired fellow named Johann Sebastian Bach, and a female Old One named Amy Beach. There were pages missing from the book, though, and I supposed there were other musicmakers among the missing.

I turned back to the picture of Haydn and sat staring at it for many minutes. I was so engrossed in it that at first I didn't hear the moaning issuing from somewhere in the house.

And then I did.

These were the same sounds I had heard nearly every night since staying in Newton's home. If I had not come to take them for granted, I had long ago assumed they were produced by strange Newton himself—perhaps bemoaning the loss of the daughter in whose room I slept. He had admitted her loss once during dinner, after an extra glass of wine, but then offered no explanation. The next time I had broached the subject with him, he had turned cold and distant, and made it all too apparent that I was not to bring it up again.

But it was not Newton who cried, for he was not home—was, in fact, hours away, on an expedition with Merlin south of the city. The two apprentices were not home, either. They had left hours earlier on their weekly shopping chores.

I was alone in the house.

The moan came again, a mournful, distant sound.

I was not alone in the house.

I put the book back in its slot on the shelf and began my search at the far reaches of where I had been allowed in the past. I found nothing, and the sounds came from a different part of the building. Newton's own bedroom was off a second hallway near the front of the house. It was usually locked, but today it had been left open. By now the bereaved sounds had stopped, but I searched the room anyway, looking for hidden panels and doors. There were none I could find. The room was sparsely furnished compared to the rest of the house—a large bed platform without headboard or footboard, a simple red coverlet. There was a plain night table and dressing table, and a large mirror. There were no pictures on the wooden-paneled walls.

I heard a moan again, and it seemed tantalizingly nearby, though not in the bedroom.

I retreated into the short hallway and waited.

The moan came again, to my right, where the bedroom was, but now muffled.

I went back into Newton's bedroom.

When the moan repeated, I went as if drawn by a magnet and stood before the full-length mirror.

I felt along its edge, and sure enough, it drew back on hidden hinges as a door, revealing a long, cool tunnel.

"Hello?" I ventured.

I was met by silence.

I stepped into the tunnel, feeling its immediate chill. There was air circulating here. I found a vent above my head, and another a few feet farther on. It was dark, and I ended up feeling my way along the cool sandstone walls.

This tunnel had been dug into the rock that bordered the house and was not part of the main structure.

I became alarmed when the tunnel made a sudden turn. There was no light behind or before me. But then I heard the moan again, closer, and proceeded.

"Hello?" I called again.

There was an answering moan that was coincidental with my call, I was sure.

Abruptly, I found myself faced with a blank wall as wide as the tunnel.

Air moved from beneath what must be a door, a cool, steady breeze.

I knocked on the door and was met with silence.

There was no knob, no handle.

I was faced with, I thought, a moral choice at that point. This was none of my business. Whoever was behind that door was part of Newton's life and had nothing to do with me. I should not even have come this far.

Suddenly I resolved to go back, and turned around.

My path was blocked by a tall figure standing there.

"You might as well see her," Newton said.

His tone was neither surprised nor angry. He sounded

resigned. He moved around me and did something to the door, which opened with a hiss. A dull light, bright in comparison with the darkness of the tunnel, issued forth.

"Please follow," Newton said quietly.

We were in an antechamber, and a second door led to the main room. It was chilly to the point of being cold, and the same faint yellow light filled this second place. There was a bed similar to the one in Newton's bedroom—in fact, the room was a duplicate of it, down to the full-length mirror and the dressing table, which held a framed picture of a feline unknown to me, short and middle-aged with a grim, almost distrustful face.

The bed was empty. But a chair faced the mirror, and in it sat, I could see by the mirror's reflection, a very old woman, seemingly asleep. I had expected perhaps Newton's young daughter, but had been mistaken.

The woman's eyes opened, and she stared at the mirror and moaned. Then she fell into troubled slumber again.

"She is my wife, Alma," Newton said. He had not taken a step toward the woman but stood regarding her, I thought, with a mixture of pity and disgust.

"What's wrong with her?" I asked.

"Everything," Newton said in the same even tone. "She refuses to face the world."

I could tell that there would be more, so I said nothing.

"When our daughter died last year," Newton went on, "Alma became increasingly withdrawn. At first she refused to leave the house, and then she refused to leave our bedroom. And then, finally, she refused to leave her chair. The doctors could do nothing for her, and finally they gave me the choice of keeping her here permanently or sending her to an institution. I had this room built as an exact duplicate to our bedroom, and here she stays. She is attended to, and, despite an occasional moan, usually in the night, this is how she exists."

"It must be horrible for her," I said, shocked.

Newton turned to regard me. "In some ways she is the lucky one."

I was further shocked at his tone, which sounded almost cold.

"How can you say that?" I replied. "The woman lost her daughter; it must have been a terrible thing to bear."

He was staring at me. "Her brother Talon killed our daughter," he said, and left the room.


AT DINNER THAT NIGHT HE TOLD ME THE REST OF THE story. I noticed that he drank more than his usual measure of wine. The stewards were almost constantly at his elbow with the bottle.

Finally he told them to leave the bottle with him and withdraw, which they did.

"You must understand something," he said with a slight slur in his speech. "My wife's family was fiercely loyal to the monarchy. Her family is one of the oldest in northern Mars. The king was one small step lower than a god to them. When the monarchy was dissolved by Augustus of Argyre they did everything they could to reinstate it, providing money and support, and, when necessary, soldiers to the monarchists, the F'rar included. This is one of the reasons why the F'rar trust me, even though they are unaware that I was never in agreement with my wife. In those days I mostly avoided the issue. I had my work to keep me busy. This, of course, was before the days of the secret Science Guild, when science could be done openly.

"But when our daughter Penelope came of age, she

became a staunch republican, which infuriated Alma and especially her brother Talon, who was working with me at the university at the time. Despite his politics, Talon and I were very close. He was brilliant. But his disapproval of his niece's positions bordered on the obsessive. Not only did Penelope support the Republic with her words, but also with her inheritance."

He stared through his wineglass for a moment, lost in recollection. "This dinner table was an unhappy place for a long time. The arguments they had . . ."

He put his glass to his lips and drained it, then reached for the bottle and refilled his glass.

"When Augustus was assassinated, things only became worse. My wife and her family supported the monarchists, of course, and Penelope followed the rallying cry of the republicans. I was powerless to reconcile them. Soon there were no dinners at all, and then, when the F'rar reinstituted the monarchy by violence last year, Penelope went off to fight them. . . ."

Again he stared off into a painful place.

"Penelope came home once, after the war began. The quarrels were even more furious and embittered than before. And then, while in a fit of madness, rather than let her go back to the fighting, my brother-in-law poisoned his own niece. Penelope died in my arms, screaming in agony. And her mother soon lost her mind."

He stared at his paws and then took another drink. Then he looked up at me.

"I was insane with grief. The monarchy, to my mind, was responsible for the death of my daughter. Even though he was dead, I blamed Augustus for my problems. As I said, I was mad. Augustus had a daughter named Haydn, and I swore that if I ever got the opportunity I would do to her what had been done to my own flesh and blood in his name."

Wearily, he reached into his tunic pocket and drew out the box I had seen him with the first night I stayed here. He opened it and drew out the delicate needle, half filled with blood, within.

"I obtained this from you after our first dinner. You may remember the pinprick you felt when you sat in my most comfortable chair. As I told you, we do many things in the Science Guild. Blood analysis is one of them." He was barely whispering, staring at the needle.

"You suspected all along," I said.

"I was sure almost from the beginning." He put down the box holding the needle, pulled his wineglass to his lips, and looked at me blearily. "But I cannot harm you, Haydn. I have gotten over my grief, and you helped me do it. I know now what my daughter was fighting for."

His eyes lost their cloudiness and became hard. "And I must tell you this. Talon escaped my wrath with much scientific knowledge, which he took to the F'rar. Of this I am sure. He is a dangerous and brilliant man, an expert in ballistics and atmospherics, and he took many secrets with him. He is no doubt developing them into weapons for the F'rar as we speak."

"Was that his picture on the dressing table in your wife's room?" I asked.

"Yes."

Almost on cue, the mournful sound of his wife's moan echoed through the house. Newton grinned, and it was like the grin of a death's-head.

"Do you like the way she sounds?" he said.

•   •   •

THE NEXT MORNING IT WAS AS IF THE PREVIOUS evening had never occurred. Newton had breakfast with me (I didn't touch my food) and then accompanied me across the garden to the guildhall. I was put in Merlin's charge for two hours, and tried to stay awake (I had had a very bad sleep in Penelope's bed) and listen to her frankly tedious lecture about igneous rocks and basalts and ancient floodplains.

Newton came for me near noon, and I accompanied him to the door leading to the chamber below, which was open again. We passed unmolested into the tunnel, and the door slid shut behind us. Newton had almost returned to his old self, with a touch of ironic smile on his lips.

"You remember your unauthorized peek down here? I thought you might like a closer look."

I said I would.

At the end of the tunnel the far door was already open, and we passed into the vast chamber.

It was noisy today, and I noticed that the sleek black shape I had seen on my first visit was gone. In its place was a shorter craft, also black, tapered at one end with a hatchway open.

As we approached, a head popped out of the hatch and regarded us.

"Ah, Peter, this is . . . Ransom," Newton said, making introductions.

Peter reached out a paw, covered in grease. "Pleased to . . . sorry!"

He wiped the paw on the sleeve of his coveralls, and this time I shook it.

He jumped out of the opening and stepped aside. "Care to have a look?"

"Yes." Since Newton made no move to step forward, I

did so and studied the inside of the structure. There were two seats, and gaggles of wires held in bundles. In front of the seats, I noticed, was a thin, wide window.

"What is it?" I asked, withdrawing my head.

Peter began to speak, but Newton hushed him.

"Come, Ransom," he said, leading me away to a corner of the theater where very loud work was going on. It looked like the large, sleek craft I had seen had been split into sections, and workers were welding canisters into one of them.

"Some sort of airship?" I guessed.

"Yes. And not a dirigible," he replied, correctly gauging my astonishment.

*"A flying ship?"*

"Yes. The fuel is still the greatest problem, but we are working on it. That book you brought us is already helping greatly."

I was still staring at the black shape, a huge body with wings like a bird, in wonder.

"We know it was done in the past, by the Old Ones," Newton explained. "Certain expeditions have uncovered artifacts of some of those ships, and we've extrapolated from that. We have some very good minds here, as you know."

"A flying ship."

"Yes." He almost laughed. "I wanted you to see this. Who knows? Perhaps one day we'll fly to the stars!"

He stopped himself, and his demeanor became serious.

"Tomorrow," he said, "you will accompany me and a few others on a large expedition to the oxygenation station near Arabia Terra. I mentioned it to you weeks ago. The trip will take almost two days. It will be dangerous. The F'rar are fighting rebels near the mountains at the moment, and we will have to be careful. A writ of free passage, which I will obtain from Carson tonight, will get us only so far. We will be passing into other jurisdictions. But I want you to come with us."

"I'd be happy to."

"Good," he said. "Now let me show you the rest of this facility. . . ."

THAT EVENING NEWTON STAYED UP VERY LATE OIL-ing Carson and obtaining the needed writ. To my surprise Newton called me out of his study late in the evening and introduced me to the fat F'rar, who was very drunk.

"My, my!" Carson said, taking my paw in his rough one and bowing. He held my paw a little too long. "Where, my dear Newton, have you been hiding her?"

"She has been away. But she will be traveling with me to Arabia Terra tomorrow."

"Ah, Arabia Terra. A terrible place. But it will be bright-ened by such beauty." He was still holding my paw. New-ton stepped forward and extricated it from Carson and, with a deft smile, turned me toward the hallway.

"You should get a good night's rest, my dear. We'll be starting early."

As I walked away he turned quickly to Carson, who was still watching me.

"We really should get that safe-passage document out of the way. . . ."

The fat F'rar nodded, and when Newton produced a newly filled glass of brandy for him he said, "Ah! Yes!" and took it.

As I walked down the hallway to Penelope's room I

heard Carson say, "You really should not hide your mistress like that, Newton. . . ."

I WAS ROUSED EARLIER THAN NEWTON HAD PROMised the next morning.

"We should leave before dawn," he explained. "Once we get away from Sagan we will be relatively safe from Carson's eyes. I wouldn't want him to get any second thoughts when he wakes up with a hangover later this morning."

"Why did you introduce me as your mistress to Carson last night?" I asked.

He smiled. "It is all very chaste, I can assure you, Haydn. Your presence with me had to be explained. So for the next few days, you will be my mistress. There is another reason, which I will not tell you about now."

I looked at his enigmatic face, knowing that if I asked he would not tell me.

TO MY SURPRISE, THIS EXPEDITION WAS MOUNTED almost like one of Mighty's caravans. There were three steam motor vehicles, one of them larger than anything I had yet seen, as well as two horse-drawn carts bearing supplies and numerous guards on horseback. I counted twelve members of the party altogether, including Merlin and two of his assistants. Old Soler was there to bid me farewell, though she wasn't going with us.

She took both of my paws in her own. "Have a safe journey, my dear!" she said. "And I must say, that book you brought us has provided us with invaluable knowledge." She turned to Newton, already sitting in the lead vehicle, a monstrous motorcar on huge wheels. "Do take care, Newton."

"We will."

I climbed in beside Newton, and Soler waved as we pulled away.

"Why did she come to see us off? It was as if we are not coming back."

"It's a dangerous trip," Newton replied cryptically.

HIS WORDS WERE PROPHETIC IN THE SHORT TERM. WE had not gone half an hour out of Sagan when two F'rar airships swooped down at us like fat vultures and landed with a bump, halting our caravan. I expected Carson to emerge from the gondola of the lead ship, but when the door opened and the ramp was thrown down, it was a cruel-looking F'rar who emerged. He was tall and thin, looking like a vulture himself, and he wasted no time. I felt Newton stiffen beside me.

"Say nothing," he whispered, and then he reached into his tunic and produced a sheaf of papers as the unsmiling F'rar stopped by the vehicle's door.

"Get everyone out," he ordered Newton and three of his own cohorts who also had emerged from the gondolas. Instantly the F'rar began to pull things out of the back of our truck and the other vehicles, and lined up our guards and Merlin's people.

Newton said, "Hello, Ceres," trying to keep his voice light, but even I could hear the tension in it.

Ceres glanced up from the papers and gave Newton a look as if he were on a glass slide under a microscope. "You might be able to pour honey down Carson's throat, but not mine," he said. His voice was devoid of inflection.

He turned his attention back to the papers, adding, "Carson was feeling rather poorly this morning, so I thought I should check into what exactly he signed last night."

"You'll find everything in order," Newton replied.

"I'm sure I will. If I thought otherwise I would have burned your caravan to cinders from the air. This says you're going on a scientific trip to Arabia Terra?"

"That's correct."

"Arabia Terra is outside of our . . . control at the moment. You are aware of that?"

"Carson mentioned it. We are well armed."

Ceres said nothing.

One of his men ran up with something in his arms. "We've searched the vehicles and subjects, sir. Mostly scientific junk, and the men have standard weapons. Two rifles and swords and arrows. But I found this."

He held it up proudly, like a trophy. It certainly did look like a weapon, with a long thin silver muzzle and a block of switches on the stock end.

Ceres looked it over idly. "What is it, Newton?" he asked.

"A ground analyzer. It bounces sonic—"

"I didn't ask for a lecture. What does it do?"

"It measures the depth of various rock layers—"

"Why?" Ceres had ceased scanning the papers and had his cold, level stare on Newton.

Newton looked almost flustered. "To see how deep they are!"

"Why?"

Newton made to get out of the vehicle. "Let me show you—"

"Never mind," Ceres said, cutting him off. He turned to his underling. "Put it back. It's nothing."

The disappointed F'rar turned and trotted off with the instrument.

Ceres continued to look at the papers, and then he suddenly tossed them back into the vehicle onto Newton's lap. "You may go on. Get yourselves killed if you like. If I were you I would wait until the Arabia Terra area is under our wing. It won't be long. It is inevitable."

Without another word he turned and walked back toward his airship, shouting to his men, "Let them go!"

In another few moments they had climbed aboard and were back in the air.

As we started up again, Newton said to me, his voice holding some of the worry he must have held in with great effort during the interrogation, "You don't know how close that was."

PITCHING CAMP WITH THE SCIENCE GUILD WAS EASIER and more luxurious than it had ever been with Mighty. When it came time, Newton merely found a suitable spot, gave the signal to stop, and five minutes later we were surrounded by a little town. Four boxes were hauled out of our truck, each with a button on one end that, when pushed, produced a huge tent. Heaters were installed, food prepared on portable stoves. Battery-driven electric light provided illumination. The only thing I didn't understand was the system of four blue stakes that were driven into the ground just outside camp, forming a square at their corners.

"I'm surprised Ceres didn't confiscate these," Newton explained when I asked about them. "Likely, one of his morons thought they were survey markers. In a way they are."

"What do they do?"

He brought me to one of the tents, where a table had been erected against one long wall. There was much equipment on the table. I recognized some of it, but not the blocky machine with a round green face in front of which sat an intent young fellow.

"Activate it," Newton said, and the young man nodded and threw a switch. The round green face began to glow, and strange flowing shapes moved across it.

"Just birds, and a small animal or so," the man reported.

"Let me know if we're bothered by anything more substantial."

At that moment I heard the squawk of a flock of birds traveling overhead.

"A kind of sentry," Newton explained to me. "We've been working on it for a long time. Those four blue stakes send out a signal that is shown on the screen. It works up to a distance of nearly a kilo. If anything—or anyone—enters, we'll know it."

"The rebels could make great use of something like this," I said.

Newton replied, "Yes, I'm sure they could. I'm sure the F'rar could also. We can be thankful that Talon wasn't working on it." His face darkened. "But he was working on other, deadlier things. . . ."

The young man turned suddenly to Newton. "Something large to the northwest."

Newton bent to study the screen, which now showed a fuzzy wide blip, deeper in color than the surrounding green, along one edge.

"It's not man-made. It looks like—"

"A harlow," the operator finished for him. There was just a touch of fear in his voice.

"A harlow," I said in wonder. A near-mythical beast, big as the truck we had driven in, and tenacious beyond reason.

"A little south for one of them, but it could be," Newton said. "I imagine the F'rar doings have uprooted all kinds of natural order." To me he said, "Come with me."

I took a final glance at the green screen, which showed the beast well within one kilometer now.

"Merlin!" Newton called as we went outside. The diminutive geologist, seated at a nearby table and eating with her assistants, hurried toward us.

"Yes?"

"Get the 'ground analyzer' immediately. And find Postelain. He's a biologist and will enjoy this. I think we're about to be visited by a harlow."

Merlin's eyes widened.

"Hurry," Newton added. "We'll be at the northwest corner."

The geologist scuttled off.

Five minutes later a crowd had formed between the northern and western blue stakes. A distant rumbling was just audible, but growing stronger by the moment. The sun had gone down, purpling the distant mountains, but one of the peaks looked to be moving.

"Maker in the sky, look at the size of that thing!" one of Merlin's assistants said in awe.

The fellow who had been manning the screen ran up and said to Newton, "Less than half a kilo—and he's coming straight at us!"

"I'm sure he is."

Just then two workers arrived with the ground analyzer and set it on a tripod. It still looked like a weapon to me. Even more so now.

One of the workers fiddled with the stock end, throwing switches and looking suddenly nervous.

"The power seems to be down," he reported to Newton.

"Oh, dear."

The distant sound was growing, a rhythmic *chug-boom chug-boom*.

Another worker ran off, and appeared a minute later with a heavy-looking box with a strap handle attached. He set it down under the tripod and ran a wire with a plug on the end up to the ground analyzer's control panel.

He plugged in the wire, there was a reassuring hum, and two dials lighted on the instrument panel.

"I would aim it a bit high," Newton suggested.

The two men, busy as they were, immediately adjusted the angle of the muzzle, pointing it higher.

"Anytime you like."

There was a visible gasp as the *chug-boom chug-boom* sound grew very loud. Now there was a silhouette growing to the northwest, starting to fill the sky in front of us.

"I would fire now," Newton said, his voice taking on a bit of urgency.

The two workers were still fiddling, but then one of them cried "Go!" and threw a switch.

Nothing happened.

My ears were filled with a thunderous roar: *CHUG-BOOM CHUG-BOOM*.

"Again!" Newton ordered.

The silhouette in front of us became a shadow and then suddenly a real thing: a huge, roaring monster bearing down on us, big and angry enough to crush the entire camp. . . .

"Now!"

The switch was thrown.

I involuntarily shouted as a blast of light brighter than the sun erupted with a high hissing sound from the muzzle of the instrument. There was a second blinding light greater than the first, and the monstrous beast, caught in the act of leaping, gave a mournful keening scream and fell with a thudding crash to the ground just in front of us. It gave a single long defeated breath, which I felt hot and beast-sour on my face, it was so close. And then it was utterly still.

The night returned to quiet, and the stars were once again the brightest points of light above the silent distant mountains.

A collective breath was let out. Merlin was already scrambling out of the camp to examine the beast. She turned a bright electric flashlight on which Newton, fearing it would broadcast our location, immediately made her extinguish in favor of a hand lantern. Unable to dampen my curiosity, I joined her.

"They say that hundreds of thousands of years ago, these beasts roamed in packs that could destroy a town," Merlin said, playing the weak light over the rough brown hide of the beast. It was mottled and pitted, and still warm to the touch. We slowly circled, examining first the tail, long and thick and whiplike with a flare of black fur on the tip as wide as a feline's head, and then the tufted ridges along the spine and crown and finally the massive head, tufted and ridged, the black, empty eyes big as eating bowls and the mouth lined, top and bottom, with massive teeth, the underjaw anchored with two tusks, not white as in pictures but stained and streaked with dried blood and the leavings of many killed beasts. The snout was long, the same color as the tail, a hoselike object known to crush victims with its encirclement.

"Amazing," Merlin said again and again. She bent her head close to look into the mouth, where the dark red tongue lolled. She backed away quickly at the stench, as did I.

"This fellow ate not long ago, and did not believe in brushing his teeth."

"He is magnificent in a way," I commented.

"Oh, yes. The king of Mars in his time. But that is long past. These tusks still bring a queen's ransom in some quarters. There are old folk tales . . ." She blushed, evident even in the weak light.

I laughed. "You mean their supposed amorous properties when ground into powder?"

"Well, yes."

"Old wives' tales?"

"We will take them with us, regardless." She shrugged, her blush receding as another point of interest caught her eye.

My curiosity sated, I went back to the camp.

Newton was standing, arms folded, looking thoughtful.

"We will have to move on tonight, I'm afraid," he said.

"Why?"

He nodded his head toward the downed beast. "That prize will bring visitors of all sorts."

"Such as . . . ?"

"Other predators, smelling meat. Or worse. Baldies, perhaps."

I told him that Merlin had noted that the beast had eaten recently.

"Then there's no time to waste."

He gave orders. Soon we had broken camp, leaving the tuskless carcass of the killed beast behind. Already, while we had done our work, scavengers, birds, and scuttering things had darted in to take a taste of the fallen monster. As we drove away I heard something larger and breathing heavily hit the body with a thud. I shivered, thinking of what it might be, wondering if these gargantuan animals ate their own kind. For the first time I was thankful for the motor vehicle, imagining what would happen if one of the creatures overtook a horse and rider.

I thought Newton would make camp again. But instead we drove all night, stopping just before dawn to sleep in what I was told was a secure spot close to our goal. Once again the perimeter was set up, but I was asleep before it was finished, having done my own chores and, secure with the protection we had and exhausted, set up my own blanket to curl up on under the stars. I was reminded as I closed my eyes of all the nights I had slept this way while traveling with Mighty.

The ground felt suddenly soft, and I slept like a kit.

# ⊰ CHAPTER 15 ⊱

THE DAWN WAS WELL PAST WHEN I AROSE. OR
rather was roused from sleep by Merlin, who was tapping
me all too gently on the shoulder.

"You couldn't wake a mouse like that, Merlin," I commented, yawning myself out of a wonderful dream, something to do with floating on a cloud over the massive
volcano Olympus Mons.

She was looking at me curiously and skittered back,
pulling her hand away.

"You have the oddest look on your face, Merlin," I said.

She tried to speak but could only stutter, "I t-t-tried it."

"Tried what?"

"This morning, th-th-thinking to make use of my time,
I w-w-woke early and sh-shaved a bit of the harlow tusk
and ground it and put it in my tea. . . ."

I held my laughter in check.

"Y-Y-You're the only other female in camp!" she cried in despair. She was exhibiting all the effects of lust, and her eyes darted to the many males walking to and fro. "What am I to do, Ransom? What am I to do?"

"Let us hope that the effects are short-term, Merlin," I began, but she suddenly rose and ran off, lamenting, "What have I done?"

Shaking my head and smiling, I broke my meager camp and joined Newton, who had already eaten, but who lingered over a cup of his own coffee, devoid of enhancement, I trusted, while I ate. I then took out one of my precious cigarettes and lit it.

Newton studied me. "We've done some research on those tobacco sticks," he said laconically. "They may not be good for your health."

"And being attacked by a harlow is?" I joked.

Camp was breaking around us.

He grunted, changing the subject. "We haven't far to go," he said. "And it's just as well, because we are being followed. I don't know by whom, but it's very bad luck. That harlow attracted far too much attention last night."

I thought of Merlin and the beast's tusks but said instead: "Are you worried?"

"Yes. But it would be just as dangerous to turn around at this point as to go on. When we get to the Arabia Terra station it will afford us some protection if we need it."

I mentioned that with the weapon I had seen in operation last night, he should have little to worry about.

"Have you ever seen a Baldy attack?" he asked, dead serious.

"No. And in the picture books they're depicted almost comically."

"There's nothing comical about them. And there is no

such thing as one Baldy. If you see one, there are usually thousands, traveling like wild animals."

His worry was palpable, and I hurriedly finished my cigarette.

He was already giving orders, and soon we were on our way.

THE VAST PLAINS OF ARABIA TERRA STRETCHED BEFORE and below us like an endless carpet of red and green. It reminded me much of my native country in the south, with the exception of the cold-looking mountains to the north, ice-tipped even at this time of year. But the plain itself was inviting, rolling hills and soft valleys filled with vegetation and dotted with blue lakes looking like shimmering coins from a distance. Newton pointed east to what at first I took to be a natural structure, a hill taller than the rest.

"The station," he announced, handing his spyglass to me, and now the lines of what I took to be a hill resolved into a structure similar to the one I had visited, though on a massive scale.

"It looks much larger than what I saw," I told him.

I continued to study. "And much more intact."

"There was a time we thought we could bring it back to life," Newton said. "There is a lot of equipment still in working order."

A thrill went through me, thinking of those massive stacks, ten of them intact, as I counted, bellowing their production into the atmosphere, the engines humming mightily, lights making the station a glowing beacon at night.

I lowered the spyglass. "I can't wait to see it."

The trip took a good portion of the morning and part of

the afternoon, but by the time the sun was lowering, the structure was rising before me like a towering peak. Its scale was massive, making the one I had been in nearly insignificant.

"The one in Meridiani was tiny compared to this," I said.

"Impressive, isn't it?"

We drove through a huge gate under a stone archway. The iron gates were rusted permanently open. There was debris, but overall the place looked well preserved. There were many more buildings than I expected: freestanding structures as well as rows of blockhouses that Newton explained contained bunks as well as what must have been at one time shops for the station's large population.

"We estimate that at one time up to ten thousand Old Ones resided here."

"I'm surprised Jeffrey never found remains," I replied.

"He looked, but the soil is not suitable for fossilization."

It occurred to me that I had not seen Merlin since that morning.

As I opened my mouth to ask Newton about it he abruptly stopped the vehicle and got out.

"This is where we start," he announced.

The caravan came to a halt. We entered, under another huge archway and open door, to a room huge in scale but similar to the one in Meridiani: offices; machines of every sort; tall pillars; and wide, boxy structures.

Newton gave orders, but they were not what I had expected.

"It sounds like you're fortifying this place rather than exploring it."

"Come with me," he said, and strode toward the far end

of the building, where a set of stairs led up to the catwalk overhead.

Our boots clanging on the metal stairway, we ascended. I followed across a bridge, trying not to look down. Newton stopped and mounted four metal steps to a trapdoor overhead. He pushed it open and I followed him out.

The afternoon was moving toward dusk. It was cool on the roof, which was flat and expansive. It made me feel like a small creature. Newton marched with purpose to the far wall.

When we reached it he stopped and pointed to the west, from where we had come, and then to the north.

The fields and valleys and hills were covered with tiny white moving things, like maggots.

"We would look as small and insignificant from here," Newton said. "Those are Baldies."

There were thousands of them making their way toward us. The nearest was just over the hill we had topped not half an hour ago.

"Our scout saw one of them early this morning as we broke camp. A second scout never returned."

"What can we do?"

"Fight them, for as long as we can."

I had seen many things in this feline's eyes over the time I had spent with him, but this was the first time I had ever seen something like fear.

"There's no hope?"

"There is always hope," he answered. "But you must understand that they will never give up. By now they know our numbers, and they know that we have the harlow tusks. You might conclude that if we left the tusks for them they would be assuaged and leave us. But the tusks are only their prize for killing us. Even without them they would have attacked us. If we had turned around for home last night they would have overrun us on the road and destroyed us then. Our bad luck was to cross paths with that harlow. From that moment on I feared this would happen. The F'rar brag that they have eliminated the Baldies in this hemisphere, but as in most things they lie."

We made our way back down through the trapdoor and to the floor of the building. The weapon on its tripod had been set up facing the door. Various loose machines had been dragged into position around it to form a defensive wall. This stretched out to either side in a curve back into flanking positions. Metal bars and tools were being stacked at ten-meter intervals behind the wall.

"We will fight here as long as we can," Newton explained. "It will be hand-to-hand at some point, I'm afraid. Are you up to this?"

"I will do what has to be done. I trained during my time with the nomads."

"Good. Our weapon will buy us some time. Baldies attack in waves, and if we can keep our little 'ground analyzer' charged, we will take care of them as they come at us. It will give out at some point, unfortunately.

"When we have exhausted our abilities out here," he continued, "we will retreat into a fortified room in the back." He pointed toward the rear of the building, well behind the artificial wall, at a room that looked small and cramped but was without windows.

"And then?"

"And then we will wait for them to get in at us." He paused, and said the next words softly. "And they will."

• • •

IT OCCURRED TO ME THAT I HAD NOT BEEN IN BATTLE
before. I had learned much from Mighty, and some from
the Science Guild, but I had never been tested. I thought
ironically that this was evident in my placement, far on the
right flank with, I thought, some of the weaker-looking
members of our party.

As I waited, a pile of tools and rusted steel rods in front
of me as weapons, Merlin appeared, looking sheepish.

"The effects lasted exactly four hours and a quarter. Can
you forgive my foolishness?"

I grinned. "Of course, Merlin." She still would not meet
my gaze so I added, "After all, it was a good experiment,
wasn't it?"

She brightened immediately. "Yes! It was the strangest
thing. I've noted it in my journal. As if a wave of something not quite myself came over me. It was quite shocking.
And then, of course, I lost control of myself completely. . . ." She began to blush. "There was a fellow from
the lower rank of apprentices . . ." Her blush deepened.

"You will be able to write it up, Merlin. It will make
quite a paper."

"Yes—"

At that moment, the Baldies attacked.

Nothing appeared under the archway immediately.
There was a sound, first, a high, keening screech that reminded me, in much higher register, of the bellowing
sound of the harlow as it charged. And then they came in
all at once, from both sides—a tide of white, screaming,
naked bodies and flashing teeth and claws. Unarmed,
which was remarkable, they still sent the ice of fear
through my veins.

Not exactly hairless as they appeared in pictures, I
noted. There were thick white patches of fur around their

genitals and under their arms, and their heads, though nearly bald, showed tufts of the same. Their eyes were large, and either very pale blue or light red, almost pink. Their strange tails whipped nervously this way and that as they advanced.

As they filled the doorway, our weapon went off with a flash. When I regained my temporary blindness the entryway was filled with writhing or dead, deformed bodies. It stopped the rest only for a moment. Without a glance at their fallen comrades, they climbed over the stricken and attacked. They did not go for the center but charged straight for the right flank, where Merlin and I and two others stood firmly rooted.

The next half hour, or hour, or five hours, or full day, was a blur of screaming, charging, white vampirish bodies. The first of them came straight at the barricades, some impaling themselves senselessly on the protuberances in front. But this madness became almost instantly understandable when those behind them used the dead as climbing pegs to get to the top of the barricades. The first I struck down with a blow from the long, rusted iron bar in my hand. His head caved in like a kawilla melon with a sickening wet sound. He fell back with a dull screech against those behind him. Merlin was having trouble, and I turned to strike another as it climbed over the top of a barricade. It fell dead and twitching between us.

"Merlin, to your right!" I shouted, and the little geologist turned in time to meet a screaming baldy head on. The creature was on her with all fours and teeth, but I kicked it away and then the soldier to Merlin's right dispatched it.

But there came others, endless others. A new wave replaced the old and mostly defeated one. Once again

Newton's weapon flashed, and more dead white bodies filled the doorway. But as others climbed the growing mountain of carcasses, others behind them pulled the dead away like so much cordwood and tossed their fellows aside. I glanced to the left. The middle was being attacked now, as well as the left flank. Yet another wave of screaming things poured through the archway and at us. I lost my rusted bar and reached down for another. When this was lost in the chest of an enemy, I used another and then another. Newton's weapon flashed again, and after recharging, again.

Two creatures jumped from the top of the barricade wall onto Merlin, who cried out as their claws sunk into her. I fought one off but the other was tenacious. I saw the flash of its long dagger teeth sink deep into the little scientist's back and withdraw, red as soil.

Merlin collapsed. I beat the second creature off her even as it sunk its teeth into her again, howling in rage and triumph.

The weapon flashed. But something went wrong and in the middle of its discharge this time. There was a huge fizzling sound and then a dull explosion. I glanced quickly left and saw the middle breached, a mass of white bodies climbing unopposed over the barricade.

"Pull back!" I heard Newton's distant, shouted command. "Fall back to the room!"

I glanced quickly up: one of the things was glaring at me with its huge pink eyes as it jumped from the top of the wall. I thrust my weapon, another rusty rod, up and it screeched in agony as the bar drove through it.

I bent to take Merlin and began to drag her backward over the floor toward the distant room.

The wall was exploding in height all along its length as

Baldies climbed up and up over the bodies of those under-neath, and began to drop down onto our side.

Someone took Merlin from the other side, and then lifted her away from me.

"Run, Haydn!"

It was Newton. The two of us turned and ran for our lives to the open doorway of the room.

Behind us, Baldies were tearing at the remains of the weapon on its broken tripod, howling in triumph, leaping onto the bodies of the dead and fallen.

"Keep running!"

The doorway drew near, and I looked back once more. We had been seen, and Baldies all along the line of battle were pointing and screeching and now chasing us.

The doorway was suddenly there, and I ran inside. Newton was close behind. There were three others already inside, and now Newton put Merlin on the floor and looked out.

"Hurry!" he shouted, scanning the battle line.

Another of our number came inside, and then one more. Newton pushed the door shut, and locked its meager lock.

"Help me barricade it!" he shouted.

We pushed whatever furniture was in the room—a desk, an empty bookcase, a cabinet—against the door, just as the first wave of screaming Baldies hit it.

It moved slightly with the blow.

"I don't know how long we have," Newton announced glumly as a sudden hush in activity left us dazed and ex-hausted.

I sat on the floor beside Merlin, whose breathing was ir-regular, a series of little gasps. She came into and out of consciousness, but suddenly she gasped and her eyes opened wide.

"Check the meter! Check the meter!" she shouted to some unseen apprentice.

There was a huge thump against the door, and the creak of our piled furniture moving incrementally back.

"Merlin?" I said in a soothing voice. "Can you hear me?"

She focused on me. She seemed to know me for a moment, but then she gasped again in pain. Her eyes lost their focus once more. "Check . . . !" she cried weakly, and then was gone.

Another loud thump sounded against the door. Now there was noise to either side of us, behind the walls to the adjoining offices. There was a bang on one wall, then the other, before long a constant tattoo of rips and slams.

"They'll dig their way in at us from either side," Newton said.

I lay Merlin's body down. Newton drew me aside, away from the rest. The tiny room was filled with noise. There were two other wounded, one of whom succumbed. The other moaned softly. There were three other survivors besides Newton and me.

"This is a terrible thing for you and for all of us, and I must apologize," Newton said to me. "I had hoped that if you returned to your rightful place, as I thought you might, that you would remember your time with the Science Guild and think kindly of us. Your father never understood us, and the F'rar will use us for ill if they don't decide in their twisted wisdom to destroy us. I had hope for you. And now things will end like this. . . ."

He paused. "I must admit that I have grown very fond of you over these weeks, Haydn. No one can replace my dear daughter, but I want you to know that in your own way you have soothed an old man with a sick heart. Thank you."

I made as if to speak, but he quieted me. "Say nothing," he said. "I think you would have made a wonderful queen."

The sounds became louder. The wall closest to us trembled. Stones began to fall inward. The screeches of delight on the other side intensified. The door buckled inward, and the furniture barricade was pushed back over the floor.

"Soon," Newton intoned.

A small hole appeared amid falling stone in one wall, and then another.

A tremendous crash came from behind the door, and it opened a few centimeters. The long claws of a baldy curled in, wresting it open even wider. . . .

And then, abruptly, the claw retreated. There was a horrid keening sound outside the door.

The pounding on the walls suddenly ceased.

The keening sound increased to an agonized height and then gradually receded.

There was sudden quiet outside.

I stole a quick glance at Newton, who bore a trace of a smile.

"Finally," he said, as if it were a prayer.

There came a knock on the door.

"Anyone home?" a hearty voice, one I thought I knew, called from outside.

Newton made a motion, and the blockade was moved away.

The door opened.

The man filling the doorway looked at Newton and nodded. Then his eyes locked with mine.

"Kerl . . ." I breathed, a whisper.

"It took you long enough to get here," Newton said, and then he gave a hearty, deep, happy laugh.

# ⊰ CHAPTER 16 ⊱

"WE HAD QUITE A FIGHT OF OUR OWN THIS MORNING before we got here," Kerl explained. We were eating a meager dinner, but it felt like a feast. We had moved to another vast building on the far side of the station, leaving the battlefield, a carpet of white bodies, to the inevitable scavenger birds and beasts, some of which were edible and had been caught. The smell of roasting meat filled the air. Kerl's men were well provisioned, and had spices (ironically, I discovered later, some of them I had carried myself) and wine. Tables were festooned with simple things: candles set in makeshift holders, scavenged silverware and dinnerware in a hundred patterns, an occasional electric lantern. The Baldies, for whatever reason, had left our vehicles untouched. When I asked about it, Newton said simply, "They're only interested in feline flesh, not in things."

I could not take my eyes off of Kerl. And I knew he

could not take his eyes off of me. For propriety's sake we sat apart, on opposite sides of the table, but I knew our conversation would be passionate later. The wine, though not very good, was not dampening that feeling.

He continued his story: "We fought our way through a F'rar army east of here at dawn. Not a large one, and lucky for us they had just finished looting a town and were fat with hangovers. I had to split my forces and melt into the countryside. I had heard rumors of a Baldy incursion into Arabia Terra but had no idea they were so close or I would have gotten here sooner. By the time my scouts reached me with the news of your peril it was already noon. We rushed here as quickly as we could."

Newton, who had regained his ironic composure, said, "Barely quickly enough, I'd say."

"True."

For a second, Kerl glanced at me, and our eyes locked.

"But our queen is safe."

To my astonishment, glasses were raised and all eyes, including Kerl's, were on me.

Newton, who had, I noted, gone significantly past his usual chaste allotment of wine, said, "She comported herself splendidly, Kerl. She fought with the best of us."

Kerl said, "Her fighting days are over now."

He stood, and held his own glass high. "To Queen Haydn, the legitimate heir to the throne!"

The rest stood, and I was left with nothing to do but stand myself. I managed to mumble, "Thank you" and quickly sat down again, as embarrassed as I'd ever been.

The rest of the meal went by in a blur, with Kerl telling of his troops quickly chopping their way through wave after wave of Baldics. "I'm afraid that at least half the force fled into the hills, and may re-form at some point."

He addressed Newton. "You may want to return to Sagan immediately."

"I've already decided that this expedition is over. We'll work through the night and head for home tomorrow morning."

"Good. I'll send a contingent of my men to guard you, at least to the outskirts of the city. I'm afraid we're not quite ready to meet your F'rar friends in force yet."

"Then you'll be leaving, too?"

Kerl nodded. "We have much to do in the east."

He glanced at me again and then suddenly rose. "There is much I need to attend to."

Newton held his glass up in salute. "We can't thank you enough, Kerl."

"Until later, then."

I waited the appropriate amount of time, feigning interest in my food and listening to drunken talk, then took my leave of the table.

Newton caught my eye as I rose, and I saw a faint, ironic smile touch his lips.

He seemed to be saying, "Go. I know what you must do."


I FOUND KERL ALONE, AS I'D HOPED. HE WAS CHECK-ing his horse, talking to it, soothing it as he brushed the dust of the day from it and combed its mane.

"There, there," he whispered. "We have another long ride tomorrow, and now you must rest."

The horse made a sound like pleasure at his attentions.

"I wish I could make that sound," I said.

He turned and stood frozen, regarding me. He still held

the brush in his hand. "I imagined this conversation would take place at some point this evening."

"It was all I could do to get through dinner."

I was suddenly in his arms, and held him as if my life depended on it.

"All these months—" I began, a sob climbing into my throat.

"Shhh. At first I thought you were dead. And then I was sure you had lived through the F'rar raid at Galle. And then more reports that you had been killed by the F'rar in Schiaparelli. And then nothing but rumors . . ."

His body shook as he suppressed his own emotions.

For a moment we stood there locked in embrace.

Finally he said, "I had long given up hope when word came from Newton that you were in Sagan."

I pushed him gently away, startled. "When did you know this?"

"Two months ago."

"And you didn't send word to me? All this time while you wondered about me, I wondered about you—"

"It was unsafe. I had this day etched in my mind. And now finally it is here. . . ."

Again we embraced. This time I cried.

"Don't weep, my queen. I have much to tell you. While your people are mostly quiet at this moment, we are readying for a great battle. When you come back with me, and they see with their own eyes that you are alive, they will rise from their meek positions and the F'rar will be driven from the face of Mars."

"I am to return with you?" I asked, surprised.

"Of course. That was my reason for meeting with Newton here. It was the reason he took you with him."

I thought of the last conversation I had had with Soler, how strangely final it had seemed.

"Yes, of course . . ."

He held me at arm's length from him and smiled. "Queen Haydn," he whispered.

"I don't know if I—"

"You must. You will. You are much changed in these many months. I can see it immediately. You are stronger and more mature." His eyes looked downward. "I heard of your litter, my brother's kits. I was so sorry to hear it."

"It was a bad time." I told him of Mighty, and the many kindnesses the brigand had afforded me. And then I blurted out something I had not meant to say: "I want to have a new litter with you."

"How can you say that?"

"Now. Before the madness begins. There will be no more battles until we are wed. I want to show our people a queen with her prince."

He looked away, and from the look on his face I knew something was terribly wrong.

He whispered, almost choking the words out: "It cannot be done."

"Why not?"

"In the time when we thought you were lost, in the beginning, there was another who consoled me. We became close, and then there were other reasons. . . ."

My heart stopped for a moment. "You are wed?" I whispered.

He shook his head no, and my heart began to beat again. "Betrothed. She is the daughter of an ally in the north, the head of the Sarn clan. If I were to break the engagement now it would mean the loss of his alliance."

He balled his paws and became suddenly angry, as did I.

"More *politics*—" I nearly spat.

"Yes! More politics! It is our lot, and our destiny, I fear. It will always stand between us—"

"Yes," I said.

He looked at me curiously, and his anger drained away. "You *are* changed," he said. He wanted to touch me again as much as I wanted to touch him, and yet we remained apart.

"We are but two," I answered quietly. "There are many, many more to think of than just ourselves."

He looked into my eyes and nodded. "Yes, my queen."

I turned from him then and walked away, and though I wanted to fall to the ground and weep, my walk was steady and true.

It was only when I was by myself later, deep in the night, in the corner of the building I had claimed for myself, that I wept long and bitter tears.


IN THE MORNING I TOOK MY LEAVE OF NEWTON, after we buried Merlin outside the walls of the station. It was a sad burial, her small body placed in a lonely grave beside the others: five of our own company from Sagan and three of Kerl's soldiers fallen in battle the day before. Newton said some words I did not hear. I was thinking of my own time with the frail geologist. I would miss her greatly. When the graves were covered it was as if she had never existed, save as another ghost in my heart.

Then it was time to go. I was given a sturdy mount by Kerl. Once again it felt as if I were losing a family. The time I had spent with Newton had been more precious than I had realized. There were tears in my eyes as I bade farewell.

His own smiled was devoid of irony and held only warmth.

"This has been a good time for me, Haydn," he said. "I hope you have learned something, too."

"Much," I said. "And you needn't worry about my forgetting the Science Guild. It will be foremost in my thoughts. As will you."

He took my paws and, to my astonishment, kissed them.

"Good-bye—daughter," he whispered.

I watched his tall figure as I rode away, safe in the bosom of a marching army, toward a distant but nearing battle.

# PART THREE

# WAR

# ⇥ CHAPTER 17 ⇤

**I HAD FORGOTTEN HOW LUSH MY OWN COUNTRY** could be.

Even though we were at the fringes of the southern plains, hiding in the mountains as Mighty would, I still could feel the differences from the places I had been. I was home. It was late autumn, and yet the fields were lushly ripe with vegetation and harvest and would stay so for weeks. This had been Kerl's idea all along, to plan the ultimate uprising and battle when the heat of summer had dissipated and the cold of winter had yet to descend.

Even the desert here was different. I had been used to the dry blowing sand of the central plains, and then the strange topography and wetlands and cold, dry forests of the north. And now here I was where I had grown up. It seemed like a foreign country to me, yet one I owned.

Our camps were widespread and relatively small, with

good, quick communication between them. Some had been supplied with message machines by Newton, though sometimes the weather interfered with their use, and there was always the problem of providing electricity for them. In such times and others, there was always a fast rider at hand. This planning, I learned, had been in place long before I had ended up with Mighty.

We were heading, I learned, to a secret stronghold, a fortress that had been built in the mountains outside Huygens.

It was a shock seeing old acquaintances after such an amount of time, especially Jamie, who looked as though he had aged a decade. At first I did not recognize him when he came into my presence. He wore chin whiskers now, banishing his youthful appearance, and walked with the stoop of an old man. But his eyes were as clear as ever, and his voice rang clear as a bell.

He embraced me, and when I was startled as he spoke, I was sure of his identity.

"I'm sorry, Haydn. I mean; my queen. It is I—"

"I know who you are now. My, how you've changed!"

He nodded, studying me. "So have you! But in your case for the better."

"What happened to you?" I asked.

"I was captured by the F'rar the day you were taken by the Yern. I was"—for a moment he looked away—"tortured for a time, and then I was sent to a prison camp. They have many of them, spread mostly through the south but now in other part of Mars. It is part of their plan. They subjugate, eliminate undesirables, retain those in camps they might find useful. Eventually . . ."

His eyes held a blank, faraway stare, as if he had seen too much.

"I escaped," he continued. "I was very lucky. Doubly lucky to find my way back to Kerl." His eyes became more focused on me. "I have heard that you tried to return yourself but were unable to."

"Yes. I had an interesting time. I will tell you about it."

He bowed. "I will be happy to hear."

Our conversation was interrupted by the approach of a tall, well-dressed female of almost regal bearing. I knew immediately who it must be. As had always been his way, Jamie quietly took his leave and left the two of us alone.

"My name is Piesha," she introduced herself, bowing slightly. "Of the Sarn clan. I am to be Kerl's wife."

She made a low, graceful bow and then looked into my eyes with an open expression as we talked of everything but her husband-to-be.

I wanted to dislike her—she was taller than I, and her bearing more assured, her manner more refined. This did not mean she had no sense of humor, which was in abundance. Her high forehead, her dark gold almond-shaped eyes, her aquiline brown nose and thin red lips—she was constructed to make me feel inadequate. And yet I liked her. She had a quality of mind I instantly adhered to, a lack of guile and fawning I found refreshing. Any man would fall in love with her, and yet Kerl had not. And I found it remarkable that she did not hate me on sight, because it was obvious that she loved him with all her heart.

Politics and marriage, again. The old curse.

She was a remarkable woman.

"My queen," Piesha said in her lilting voice, "Kerl has told me something of what you have been through. It is a horrible story, yet fascinating. If there is anything I can do, I am at your service."

Again the graceful bow.

"Thank you, Piesha. I hope that we can be friends."

She saw my meaning instantly, and embraced the words for what they were—a true offer of friendship.

She smiled. "I hope so, too, my queen."

Kerl joined her, and there were a few more minutes of amiable chatter before Piesha retreated and Kerl and I were alone.

"What do you think of her?" he said.

"Do you really want to know?"

He frowned. "Yes."

I could not keep my own feelings completely under control, but I gave it my best. "You have done remarkably well under the circumstances, Kerl. Don't treat her the way I treated your brother. It will only make both of you unhappy."

He was studying me. "Do you mean that?"

"I do. We will not speak of these things again. We've already made our noble pronouncements about duty before self. I see no reason to repeat them."

"You *have* grown a lot," he said.

"I hope so. And now I would like to see what your plans are for this coming campaign."

"You need hardly concern yourself—"

I let anger show. "I was once informed by you that I would be a figurehead in this war. That will not be so. I mean to lead this army."

"*What?*" he sputtered. "That is imposs—"

My anger turned, for the first time in my life, to command. "Kerl," I said, letting ice coat the words.

Something about my changed manner froze him. "I truly don't know you anymore," he said in wonder.

"You know me well. But there is another part of me that has been honed by this long time away." I let my tone soften a bit. "How do you expect our people to fight and die for me if I'm nothing but a cowering figure hiding in a fortress tower somewhere? Will they fight for that? You want them to fight for an idea, the idea of the legitimate monarchy—but why should they if the legitimate monarchy has no real face? My father would have done as much as I. They will never put their hope in me if I am not with them.

"I learned to fight during my time with Mighty," I went on. "I fought just yesterday with Newton, when there was no choice. Today there is a choice, and I make it."

"But Haydn—"

"From now on you will address me as your queen. I appoint you counselor, as well as commander of armies. You are my first in command. I am not so foolish as to think I can plan a battle or execute a plan without expert help. I expect to get it. I will defer to you in all proper things, and you will defer to me in *all* things. Do you understand, Kerl?"

His flabbergasted look was slowly replaced by something else. "I hope this is the right course . . . my queen."

"I share your hopes. Now bring me to your war tent and show me your plan of battle."

After hesitating, he bowed his head. "Yes, my queen. But I think we may need to talk of these things again."


TO MY SURPRISE, I UNDERSTOOD MOST OF WHAT Kerl showed me during the next week, and quickly picked up much of the rest. We moved our camp twice, keeping well ahead of F'rar scouts, and would soon reach the mountain stronghold Kerl had built. I now understood what Kerl meant for us to do. The plan, on paper, was a simple one. Frane and her cohorts had spread like a thinning stain over nearly half of Mars. Their influence now extended to nearly every inhabited province, and all but the wildest clans had been at least partially subdued. What Kerl meant to do was to peel back this influence starting at its farthest, thinnest, weakest points, and then continue to push back until the F'rar were concentrated where they had started, in the city of Wells. Then an all-out battle would ensue. The insurrection would start with the sleeper cells already in place in the outlying districts, which extended, at least in the north, far past Sagan and Shklovskii at this point. Here the campaign would begin. They would be assisted by small bands of our army that had been quietly gathering for months in the far districts to aid the rebels. My old friend General Xarr was overseeing these operations and soon would return to aid Kerl and me.

Simultaneously, our own main army would battle the F'rar where we were, keeping them from crushing the weak resistance to the west. By the time the forming army in the west joined with our own, we would have enough forces to march on Wells.

"It is audacious and simple," I said, standing with Kerl and his military advisers in the war tent on the last day before heading for the fortress. "But will it work?"

Kerl smiled grimly. "You ask a commander for precognition?"

"I only ask if everything is in place."

He nodded. "As much as it ever will be. If we wait much longer, the outlying districts will be overrun completely and subdued by the F'rar, and winter will overtake us."

"You have sent out word that I will head the army here?"

"I have."

"And the reaction?"

"Skepticism."

"I see. Well, we will try to take care of that."

There was a new coolness between us, which I saw as both necessity and armor. Every time I saw Piesha, and longed to be in her place, the armor grew harder, its steel colder.

Kerl's subordinates, two lieutenants and the more than able Captain Prelan, who was one of the tallest felines I had ever seen, gave their reports and then left the tent. Kerl and I were alone in front of the maps and plans.

"There is also fear, my queen."

"Of what?"

"That if you are killed in battle, there will be nothing to fight for."

My reply was too hasty: "That is foolish."

"Is it? I speak as counselor now. I told you we would have to speak of these things again. You have no relatives. There is no direct line to the throne behind you. If you were to die, our own forces would turn on themselves, clan fighting clan for the right to succeed. It would doom the rebellion and establish Frane's claim to the throne, which she hasn't been able to do."

I could feel myself growing hot with anger. Pride was fighting reason, and the battle was all the worse because I suddenly knew he was right.

"Then—I will stay behind."

A visible flood of relief went through him. "Thank you, my queen. You have made the right decision."

"It is not an easy one, counselor."

For the first time in a week I saw a tiny smile come to his lips, though an ironic one. "None of them will be, my queen." The smile vanished. "There is another question that has come up in counsel with my staff. It is an old one, and I feel bound to bring it up with you."

"Yes?"

He hesitated. "It concerns the succession of which I spoke."

I suddenly knew why he was having such a difficult time.

"You speak of my having another litter."

He would not speak, staring at the ground, but only nodded.

"To do that, I would need to wed."

"Yes, my queen. For the good of our people."

"This is . . . something I must think about. You are a good counselor, Kerl."

When he had left I added to myself, "Too good."

GENERAL XARR RETURNED FROM THE EAST A FEW days later. I immediately summoned him.

He knelt before me with his head down, and would not meet my eyes.

"The last time I saw you, General," I said, "you were drunk."

"I wish I were dead at this moment, my queen."

"Get up, and let me embrace you."

He did so, and when I gently pushed him away I was startled to see tears on his ugly face from his one good eye.

"I haven't had a drink of red wine or anything else since that day!"

I studied his scarred face, his empty eye socket, his missing ear. "You are a good man, Xarr."

"I am a man filled with shame! I vowed to die for you,

and on that day, because I was drunk, I slept through it all! The battle, your disappearance, all of it! Later I begged Kerl to let me go after you, but you were nowhere to be found!"

"Thank you, General. I will need your help in the coming days."

His tears had dried, and he knelt before me again and bowed his head.

"I will never leave your side again until my body is cold and stiff!"

THE CAMPAIGN BEGAN TWO WEEKS LATER. WORD went out to the west by courier and, when possible, by radio machine. A few days later, word came back that full-scale revolt against the F'rar had begun. Our own forces mobilized at the fortress stronghold. Well camouflaged, it was a veritable castle carved halfway up the face of Mount Cassini. It was to be my place of safety, from which I would view the battle. The very thought of it made me grit my teeth, but it was well appointed, and its war room was spacious and up-to-date. General Xarr would stay behind also, with a small contingent of reserves.

Kerl rode out on a fine autumn morning, with Piesha beside him. Her battle dress was magnificent, red beaten armor made by her people, ornamented with the colored flowers and filigreed birds of their region in the far north. It was strong yet looked delicate. Once again I had to stifle pangs of jealousy, though I did try to have her removed from battle for Kerl's sake. The gesture was a useless one—bordering, I was informed, on insult. The Sarn clan had always fought, man and betrothed, side by side, and it would always be so.

The gates of the stronghold were thrown wide as the army left at first light. The rose-colored sun glinted off of hundreds of armored helmets and hundreds of steeds.

Kerl and Piesha turned to salute me. And then they were gone, winding down the switchbacks to the wide plain below, where the first battle would take place. From the fortress tower I could make out the F'rar army arranged in standard line.

Even before the tail of Kerl's army was out of sight, the F'rar were attacked on their flanks by the bands Kerl had assembled to the east and west. The sounds of battle, muffled and far away, filtered up to me. I was joined by Jamie, but I sent him away. I wanted to be alone. I was dressed in my finest robes, red and cream, with a beaten gold crown on my head. If they wanted a figurehead I would be one, and stand tall for them to see while they fought, while some of them died.

Kerl's army reappeared, gaining the plain below, spreading out as they did so. They were more ragtag than I realized, their weapons almost meager—some rifles, one cannon, a line of archers, with many foot soldiers carrying spears, swords, and knives.

I imagined I heard the call to charge, though I knew it was too far away to reach me.

The battle line advanced. Kerl's single cannon fired off once, then again, crashing into the F'rar line, which had unwisely split in the middle to cover the flanking attack.

Kerl's men went straight for the break, which then closed up in a pall of smoke and the faraway popping of rifles.

The smoke grew higher and wider, covering the battlefield from end to end.

It was then that I saw, streaming down from the hills to

the far west and east, a horde of white bodies on foot whose unearthly screams I could hear even from this distance.

*"Baldies . . ."* I whispered in disbelief.

The white horde disappeared into the fog of the battlefield.

The dust climbed into the air and held there like a fog.

I heard shouts around me, cries of sudden alarm.

I realized that it was not the smoke of battle at all I was witnessing, but the pall of a massive dust storm engulfing the entire field of battle.

It rolled higher, blotting out the rising sun, the sky, rolling up the mountainside like a red tide toward us.

I listened for sounds from the battlefield, but there was nothing now but the deadening sound of roaring wind. Now the first pellets of sand and dust hit me. I was thrown to my knees on the parapet as they became a flood.

Hands were under my arms, helping me to my feet.

"You must come inside!" a voice called close to my ear.

The swirling dust was so thick now I could barely see the face—it was one of my many attendants, a young girl named Beth, whose husband was a foot soldier.

"I want to stay here for them, Beth!"

"You must come inside, my lady!" she insisted. She began to drag me away.

Now I could not see my own self. The howling wind reached at me, trying to tear me away from the helping hands and out over the wall.

I fell to my knees and began to crawl toward the safety of the tower, Beth supporting me.

We made it safely inside, and with some effort Beth closed the heavy wooden door behind us.

Out of the howling wind and tearing dust, I rested on

the stairs and contemplated the frightened visage of the girl who had assisted me.

*"They are all gone!"* Beth said, sobbing.

Breathing heavily, I put my paw on her arm. "No. But the battle is uncertain now. All we can do is wait."

*"All gone!"* she repeated in horror.

I heard the wild whistle of the wind at the door behind me, the pounding hiss of building sand, and had to wonder if she was right.

# ⇥ CHAPTER 18 ⇤

**THE STORM LASTED FOR TWO DAYS. IT CONTINUED**
to intensify through the first day, until the world outside
disappeared completely.

At first we hoped for stragglers to make their way back
to the fortress, but I feared this was a false hope. At the
dawn of the second day, hopes rose when the howling
wind suddenly slackened. But this was only momentary,
and when it resumed, it was with even greater fury.

After spending time with Jamie and Xarr and others of
my advisers, who had no advice to give and only gloom to
offer, I retired to the kitchen with the cooks and two of my
maidservants. Beth had become close to me in the hours
since the battle, and I was able to give her some comfort.
Feeling useless, I availed myself of the task. The other
maidservant was her steadfast friend Masie. I found that I
enjoyed their company, especially in the kitchen, which

was in the bowels of the fortress and away from the beating howl of the wind.

"I heard tales about these here dust monsoons," Brenda, our fat cook, was saying. Though I was a queen, she held her own court in this place. She waved her spatula like a waggling finger. "Heard tell of men bein' stripped to the bones after so long as an hour in the middle of it." She nodded her head sagely.

I briefly considered telling them of my own experience with a dust storm, but thought it best to be quiet.

Beth burst into tears.

"There, there, darlin'," Bertie, the cook's skinny husband, said. "Don't you listen to ol' Brenda. She's just talkin' tales she is."

"The thing I find strange," said Masie, who was educated and wise, older than Beth and less high-strung, "is how quickly it came on. Not natural-like."

"Almost as if it were deliberate," I added, unable to merely listen any longer.

There was instant quiet in the room.

"I told all of you already to treat me as if I'm just another servant," I said.

"Pardon me for saying it, my lady, but you ain't!" Brenda replied.

After a moment's hesitation, Masie broke out in laughter, and the others followed, Bertie's own "Haw, haw!" a few decibels above the rest.

It was the first laughter I had heard in two days, and I joined it. Even Beth smiled momentarily before beginning to fret again.

"I'm so worried—"

"I have to say," I interjected, "that I much prefer the

company of this room to a war room of melancholy advisers—"

At that moment Jamie, looking haggard and even older then he had before the battle, appeared in the doorway.

"Pardon me, my queen, but a survivor has made it to the front gates."

I arose, and Beth gave a gasp. "Is it—"

Jamie glanced at her and said, "It's Captain Prelan."

"Is the storm over?" I asked.

Jamie shook his head no.

"Then how did he make it back?"

Jamie continued to shake his head no. "I have no idea. He's blind and dying. You should see him."

I followed Jamie out of the kitchen, listening to the whispered chatter of my new friends behind me, and Beth's wail.


CAPTAIN PRELAN'S FACE WAS STRIPPED NAKED AND bloody, one of his eye sockets scoured clean and empty. The other was bandaged.

He lay on a table gasping, calling in a rasping voice for water. When water was given to him he dribbled a few drops into his mouth and cried, "Dry! Dry!"

"Sit him up," I said gently.

I drew close, and took his bloodied paw in my own. "Captain Prelan, it is Queen Haydn. Can you hear me?"

He stiffened into a form of attention. "Yes!"

"Sit back, Captain. Can you tell us how you got here?"

"Crawled for . . . hours. Water!"

Once again he took a few drops and cried, "So dry!"

The doctor, who was supporting the captain's head,

looked at me and said in a low voice, "His lungs and stomach are coated with dust."

I nodded, and squeezed the captain's paw. "Do you remember anything of the battle, Captain Prelan?"

"Filthy . . . Baldies . . . fighting aside the F'rar. . . ." Again he asked for water. "The F'rar had dust masks. They knew . . ." Again, water, and now his voice was weakening. "Kerl tried to ride through the storm but . . . it followed us like a flood. . . ."

"The storm *followed* you?"

He nodded slightly, then clutched my paw tightly. "As if it were being directed. Had to come back . . . Kerl sent me . . . the F'rar know about the fortress. . . ."

"They know we are here?"

He nodded again, tried to speak, but only a croaking rasp came out. "Water, please . . ."

I looked at Jamie and the other military advisers and said, "Come with me."

"NEWTON OF THE SCIENCE GUILD INFORMED ME THAT a feline named Talon has been providing the F'rar with technology. He was an atmospherics and ballistics expert, and a traitor. They may have developed a method to produce local dust storms. Who knows what else they have developed?

"I think we can have every reason to believe that when the dust settles, the F'rar army will be standing at our gates."

"We cannot be there to meet them, Your Majesty!" General Xarr interjected. "We have only my reserves, and not enough of them! And only the old and very young beyond that!"

"I have no intention of fighting them now. But I also have no intention of being here for them to slaughter. Here is what we will do. . . ."

WHEN THE STORM BEGAN TO LIFT THE NEXT EVENING, we were ready. The previous twelve hours had been hectic ones, but everyone from my old general down to the kitchen staff performed magnificently.

The first part of the climb was the hardest, with choking dust still swirling. But with everyone properly masking their faces with the primitive but effective wet cloth Mighty had taught me, we came through intact. The mountain passes behind the fortress were numerous and easy to follow. Before long we had climbed out of reach of the dust storm. The glorious light of faint Phobos overhead filtered the night like a friendly lantern. I looked down and saw a blanket of haze looking like a pink cloud covering most of the mountain and our fortress below us. As I watched, it seemed to recede a bit.

"Talon is letting up on the storm," I said.

Beside me, Jamie nodded.

We continued to climb.

The plan was not audacious. I doubted the F'rar would follow our ragtag remains into the scattered heights of the mountain, and I was right. With our army split into hundreds of pockets, it would take them weeks if not months to root us out. As I hoped, they did not bother to try.

After twenty-four hours, and a few not-bad meals made from local roots that Brenda, who had insisted on accompanying me, turned into delicacies, I thought it safe enough to descend to one of the many promontories that dotted the mountainside. From there I could survey our former home and the battlefield beyond it. Scouts had been here from the beginning, reporting on the retreat of the dust storm and its wake. I was not surprised by what I saw through one of their spyglasses.

The fortress was pink with dust that had drifted like dirty snow up its sides. It was free now of F'rar interlopers, who had poured through the gateways at one point and then, mere hours later, retreated. They had joined their main force on the battlefield, which had then moved off to the east.

The Baldies were nowhere to be seen.

I surveyed the battlefield and saw no movement, and no sign of the great army that had left our fortress. It was a plain of drifted, silent dust, like the surface of another planet.

"I want scouts to make sure the F'rar army is gone for good. Tomorrow we will go down there."

"Yes, my lady," General Xarr answered.

That night the sweet mountain roots that Brenda cooked tasted bitter in my mouth.

THERE WAS NOT A BREEZE TO STIR THE RED DUST THE next morning. Only a small contingent came with me, since we had not many horses, and without their steady, strong legs it would be almost impossible to get through the stuff, which was knee deep in places.

It was silent now, but I could hear the silent screams of the dead in my ears. Here and there, like monuments of defiance, an arm bearing a sword, or the legs of a fallen mount, poked through the surface like a bizarre sculpture. There were many mounds, where bodies lay entirely covered. In one spot a dead soldier sat, his chest to the top of his helmet exposed, his open mouth filled with dust. Below the surface he had been pierced with a F'rar sword.

"We'll never find them all," Xarr commented.

"We won't even try."

I rode on through this petrified field of death, my heart growing heavier. I had hoped that by some miracle some had survived, that Kerl had been successful in his inherently good choice to attempt to ride completely through the artificial storm and out the other side. My mare stumbled on a buried body and I urged her forward, around the fallen soldier. My eyes were on the far side of the valley, where the red dust eventually thinned up a far hill. If only Kerl and some of his men had made it that far.

But there was nothing but this field of ghosts and swirling dust.

Xarr rode up to join me, his mount kicking red drifts aside. "What do you wish?" he asked.

I hardened my voice. "How many do we have in reserve?"

He looked surprised at my question. "Perhaps three hundred, if that many."

"And if all the able bodies are conscripted, as well as ill and infirm fit enough to fight?"

"To fight? Do you mean to pursue the F'rar army?"

I ignored his question. "Did you notice their airpower capacity?"

"They had no airships."

"Which means they relied on Talon's machine."

"My lady, even if we could pursue and catch the F'rar, the Baldies—"

I dismounted, my boots sinking into the rusty ground covering. Nearby was the extended dead arm of one of our soldiers. I reached down into the powder covering it and pulled up something long and white, a different arm whose long claws lay locked around my soldier's own.

"The F'rar lured the Baldies here and killed them, too. They were not given masks. They were not allies, but victims."

"Merciful Great One in heaven . . ."

"At what strength would you estimate the F'rar army?"

He considered this, tallying. "By sight, I would say one thousand. Perhaps as many as twelve hundred."

"Very well. Return to the fortress and strip it of everything usable for a forced march. We have wagons enough for provisions. Pack them to the brim. Send out scouts, but tell them by all means to remain unseen. We will leave at dusk and catch the F'rar before they can reinforce.

"I will lead the army."

# ⇥ CHAPTER 19 ⇤

I COULD SAY ONE THING FOR GENERAL XARR: ONCE given orders, he acted on them. If there was grumbling, I never heard it.

The setting of the sun found us heading east, pursuing the F'rar army. Scouts had found them easily, as they made no attempt to hide themselves. Having vanquished two enemy forces with one deceptive blow, they were feeling fat and happy, and had stopped to pillage what small towns lay on the way. We passed through two of these unfortunate outposts and were treated to nothing but tales of woe.

We almost overran them at a third, larger town, named Odin. It was late into the night, almost dawn, and yet their revels continued. From the hill where we came to rest I could hear their drunken shouts and the sound of music. Torchlights burned. At least one home had been set afire.

"They will never be more vulnerable," I observed, watching the raucous proceedings below.

"Do you propose to attack them now?" Xarr asked. I had learned by now that he was much better at taking orders than formulating them.

"No. But find me one feline good with explosives and another with weapons, and have them meet me here in ten minutes."

"You don't mean to go down there by yourself!" Xarr protested in horror.

"No," I said, smiling grimly. "I'll have those two experts with me."

THE EXPLOSIVES EXPERT, TO MY SURPRISE, WAS MY maidservant, Masie. "Let's just say I have many talents," was her explanation. When I explained to her what I wanted she had no trouble with it, nor with her change of clothing to nomad dress.

The weapons fellow was fresh out of the hospital, wounded in the left side but right-handed and more than ready for battle. He had more trouble with the robes but was more than willing to fight. His name was Brace.

"I hope it doesn't come to it," I instructed him, "but have your blade ready."

"Yes, my queen," he said.

With no more discussion we made our way down the hill, toward the darker end of the town.

It was almost too dark: my companions and I stepped into a trench that proved to be a latrine. To their credit, they made no protest, but I could not hide my own disgust. On climbing out the other side, I observed, "Just think of it as more camouflage."

We soon were able to test our camouflage, as a F'rar foot soldier appeared and ordered us to halt. He was very drunk, but still bore a dangerous sword and a nasty expression.

"Who are you?" he said when we halted.

Then, the wind being to our backs and toward his nostrils, he said, "Ugh! Latrine workers?"

I nodded.

"Get on with it!" he shouted, urging us past and covering his nose. "Damn it!" We heard him retch as we hurriedly passed.

"I didn't think we smelled that bad," I commented when we were safely within the town limits.

Masie, obviously disagreeing, rolled her eyes.

The lights of the officers' quarters were like beacons. They had appropriated the town hall, such as it was, and as we approached it from the rear, the smell of spilled ale almost overwhelmed our own odor. I sneaked a look through one of the windows and saw what I expected: three or four diehards still wielding flagons, the rest sleeping where they had fallen, on the floor or on tables. In one corner I recognized one figure not inebriated: Talon, the fat traitor with the piggish eyes, looking just as he had in the photograph in Newton's wife's room. Talon sat seriously discussing something with a man who bore a general's rank but who was much more interested in the ale in front of him than in his companion's words. Surrounding them were three well-armed bodyguards, very much sober.

I cursed silently. If only there had been more of us, we could have given Talon the death he so richly deserved.

We moved around the rear of the building to the side, where three horse-drawn wagons and two huge, long motor vehicles were parked. I examined each in turn and found what I hoped to find in the motor vehicles: two huge machines, long white tubes mounted with switches and dials at one end. They looked familiar.

"Mount your charges at each end and in the middle," I ordered Masie.

After examining the machines, she nodded. "There'll be nothing left but scrap," she promised.

Hearing a rise in the noise level of the building next door, I added, "And hurry!"

Fifteen minutes later she reported, "All ready. They'll go off in twenty minutes."

We drew away from the building just as a guard, looking suspiciously sober, appeared in a side doorway.

"Wait," I whispered, and watched while he poked around the spot we had just vacated.

I nodded to Brace, who was already drawing his blade, moving stealthily toward the guard, who had put his head inside the tarp.

In a minute Brace was back, and I noticed the guard stumbling, unhurt, back to the building.

"All he did was pee," he said simply, putting his blade into its sheath. "He found nothing."


WE MADE IT UP THE HILL AND BACK TO CAMP BEFORE the charges went off. After discarding our rancid clothing we immediately set off for the plain east of town, which our scouts had promised was good for battle. A small band on horse was left behind. They would drive through the town at dawn and push the F'rar army toward us, like shepherds driving a herd.

"We will see how well they fight without their machines," I said.

"And full of bad ale," Masie added.

As we reached the field of battle the charges went off, sending two dull, booming plumes of yellow fire into the dawning sky. I saw Masie frown until, a few seconds later, two more charges went off. We watched a blasted section of white tube fly into the air and break into three pieces.

"As I said, scrap," Massie stated, grinning in satisfaction.

"And now," I said, marking the peeking of the sun's edge above the violet lip of the horizon.

As if on cue, there was a woop and wild cry from our riders. Shots were fired amid shouts from the town. I watched through my glass as our little band of wild rousers tore down the streets and then out of the town and toward us.

"General Xarr, deploy your troops, please," I ordered.

"Yes, my queen," he answered, and just as the full sun topped the far hills, we were ready.

The F'rar came on, streaming out of the town wild and in disarray, just as I thought they would. They were angry and confused, half dressed and still muzzy with drink, but they formed a battle line before they met us. I'm sure their cocky commanders thought the little force that faced them head-on was a suicide stand, the remnants of Kerl's army, and would be easily overriden. They charged straight at us.

"General, flanking positions, please," I ordered.

Xarr gave the orders, and the rest of our force appeared to the right and left of the F'rar force and clamped them in a vise.

The air was filled with cries and shouts and the flashing of blades. The F'rar force never made it as far as our weak front line, so I gave the order to take the battle to them. My own blade flashed in the new sun, and soon the F'rar were calling for retreat, which was impossible, since our flankers had closed off escape behind them.

A rout ensued. In an hour the battle was over, the battlefield littered with F'rar dead, their deserters making for the hills. I ordered bands to pursue. I was particularly interested in what had happened to Talon. I had a feeling he had stayed behind.

Late in the day, after we made camp east of the battlefield, Xarr gave his report.

"Talon was not found, my queen," he said.

"Have scouting parties head west and north. We may get lucky."

"And what do we do now, my lady?"

"We pursue Kerl's original plan and keep moving east. Have you heard from any of the rebels in the west?"

"Our radio machines are limited, and no couriers have returned as yet. But the F'rar had some superior machines, and we may be able to utilize them."

"Do so. I need to know that the rebellion is rolling toward us as Kerl expected, not collapsing behind us."

"I have no doubt word of your victory today will help greatly," Xarr said. There was, I noted, a new respect in his voice. "A thousand against three hundred . . ."

"We have made a good start," I said. "But we need to build this army if we are to move toward Wells."

"My lady?" Xarr said in surprise.

"Did you think we would gain one victory and retire for the winter?" I asked.

"No, but—"

"The goal, Xarr, must still be Wells. Without that we are nothing but a rebel army that will eventually be crushed by Frane. She will turn new weapons against us or starve us out or move to annihilate us with superior force. We need help."

As I said, Xarr was good at taking orders but less useful at concocting them. I sat in thought while his confusion only grew.

"We need help," I repeated, to myself.

# ⊰ CHAPTER 20 ⊱

THE VOICE IN MY EAR WAS FAMILIAR AND AS FAR away as Deimos. There was an intermittent crackling and fading in the headset. But it was good to talk to Newton again.

"Things have been . . . interesting in Sagan," he commented. Even with the bad reception, I could hear the irony in his gravelly voice. "It was particularly interesting to watch Carson and his ogres run with their tails between their legs. I hear he is hiding in the mountains with one airship. All in all, Sagan is a free city again."

I asked him how far the F'rar had been pushed back.

"I can't say for sure. Our own twin cities are free of them for the moment, but the smaller towns between you and me are saturated with deserters. There is a reliable rumor that a great army is forming under our old friend Ceres. I wouldn't doubt it. He was always Carson's better, and now he will try to prove it. Due to sheer numbers, there were fewer rebels in waiting in the small towns than in the cities to handle such an influx of fleeing F'rar. It was, in retrospect, the one flaw in Kerl's plan."

"His plan worked all too well."

"Yes."

I then told him of our encounter with Talon, and approached the real reason for my communication.

After a silence that at first worried me, he answered, "There are certain things I can do to help you. There is a stockpile of Science Guild equipment north of you, in Burroughs. I have already sent Jeffrey to meet you there. There is much in it you will find useful. As for Talon, I would fear that he has kept his worst in reserve. It is his nature. He is heartless and soulless. I will do what I can for you here."

The signal became intermittent, before fading altogether with his final enigmatic words: "You will meet someone along the way . . ."

I spoke into a void of static: "Take care, Newton."

XARR DID NOT UNDERSTAND MY STRATEGY BUT DID obey my orders. He was a native of Burroughs and knew the way. We set out at once for the northern city, a ten-day march. It was a hard journey over much jumbled terrain. There was a rainstorm that turned the dust instantly to mud, which added nearly a day to the trip. Wildly flowing water cascaded in what had been dry creekbeds the day before. And then, as if to mock us, after a brief period of clearing late in the day, the skies darkened once more, and it began to snow. The temperature dropped twenty degrees, then ten more. Before us was the summit of an extinct volcano, Arsia Patera, which had to be traversed.

Through the howling wind of the sudden weather change, I shouted to Xarr, "Do you think it would it be best to camp here, or make the summit?"

"If we stop, we will die," he answered immediately. "Locally, we call this weather a *himrit,* which means 'teeth of the creator' in an old local language. It can last for an hour, or it can go on for days or even weeks. There is no way to tell. At the summit it will be better. If we must stop, make it there. In another two hours we will be buried in snow here."

I shouted, "Let's do as you say!"

We pushed on.

Night had fallen by the time we reached the caldera. As Xarr had predicted, the storm was less severe at the summit. We could hear it howling in the crevices and hollows below us; here, there was but a swirling of snow and a strange, foggy luminescence that had settled on the top of the mountain like a blanket. We made what camp we could. There were almost enough tents, and those who could not fit in them took the first watch. I insisted on being one of them. After much wrangling about my station, I succeeded in my wish. It was not so much out of altruism as uneasiness that I sought to participate in the first watch. I knew I would be unable to sleep with this fog around us.

Xarr kept me company for a time. We were huddled beneath a rock outcropping near the path that had led us up the mountain. He surprised me by producing a flask from deep within his tunic. It contained a spicy rum that was new to me. "For you, my lady. As I said, I have not touched a drop since the day I let you down. I keep it to tempt and remind me of my sins. It is the finest on all of Mars."

He handed it to me. He was right: it was excellent.

Xarr seemed more at ease than ever since I had met him. "There are many tales in this part of the world," he said, staring out with me at the fog, which lay nearly at our feet. Our ears were more valuable than our eyes at this point. I took a long pull from his flask and wiped my mouth with the back of my paw. "Many tales."

His hooded eyes regarded me. "Ghosts and such, my lady. My own grandfather, who helped turn Burroughs from a mining town into a city, was seen as a spirit after he passed on. I know this for a fact because I was the one who saw him."

My incredulous smile must have gotten to the old general, for he nearly bristled with indignation. "It's true! It was a night not much different from this. I was out with my father hunting rabbit and became separated from him. The sounds of his voice seemed nearby, but he was actually half a kilo away.

"And then I heard another sound."

Almost on cue, we heard something in the distance through the fog, a step or shuffle of feet.

Xarr's eye's widened. "Just like that! Only much closer. Like a man dragging a chain over the ground."

We heard the sound again, closer, and a childish tendril of fear rose up my back.

Xarr, lost in his story now, went on: "I stood rooted to my spot as if I had grown roots. The shuffling came closer and closer. And then I remembered that my grandfather had died in the mines, when an iron chain clamped around his middle that had been hauling him up a hole broke, sending him to the bottom of the shaft. And here was that same chain, drawing closer to me like a huge, heavy snake slithering slowly along the ground!"

He paused, and now I took a long drink from the flask. Xarr looked at me in surprise, and then froze at the sound we both heard out in the fog.

*"Like that!"* he whispered fiercely, pointing with a shaking claw out into the wet, white gloom. The shuffling noise I had heard was closer, somewhere down the path leading up to us.

I stealthily drew my blade.

"Go on," I said to the old general, but he was shaking his head slowly. He carefully took the flask from me and put it away. He stood next to me with his own dagger drawn.

His eyes widened with fear as something rose out of the fog in front of us, a black-hooded shape dragging something behind—

"Grandfather!" Xarr shouted, jumping out to confront the specter and at the same time shield me.

There was a commotion. The black hood was thrown back. Something behind the figure dropped. Xarr wrestled the ghost to the ground, shouting to me, "Save yourself, my queen!"

Then there was a shout of anger followed by laughter and the two figures rolling to a stop while the hooded mass stood up, looking down at the general on the ground and continuing to laugh.

"Xarr, you old fool! Are you drinking again?"

"Kerl!" I shouted.

*"Yes,"* he said, suddenly grim, lifting the poles of the litter he had dropped and bearing it to me. Behind it were three other figures, two of them stumbling blindly and holding the third for guidance.

I bent down to examine the figure on the litter, pulling back a blanket that covered the face.

I gasped.

"Yes," Kerl said, kneeling down beside me. He gently covered the ruined face, not much more than a skeleton, of his wife.

"How—" though I already knew.

The three other figures, two of which I now saw were similarly deformed, shuffled past us into camp.

"Xarr, attend to them please!" I ordered.

He instantly complied, leaving Kerl and me alone with the silent figure under the blanket.

Kerl stood looking down at the covered figure. His own face was streaked with lines of blood and healing scars. "We were lucky to get out at all. The dust cut like daggers. I covered my face immediately, but those who didn't were not well off. Eventually the dust cut away my coverings. By then we could neither see nor hear. This fog was like clear glass compared to it. I drove them through, but only a score made it with me. . . ."

His eyes were glued to the unmoving figure.

Quietly he continued, "I kept pushing them on. From the far hills we watched the dust for two days. I saw it reach the foot of the fortress, then overtake it. And when it was over I watched the F'rar charge your position. At that point I had nine useful men, and the F'rar were after us also. We managed to hide in the hills and scatter. I re-assembled whoever hadn't been hunted like dogs. What you see is what was left."

He looked from his wife to me. "By the time I reached the fortress, everyone was gone. But then I talked with Newton on the radio machine. Word of your battle to the east had reached them, and he passed it on to me. It was a great victory, my lady. I should have been there for you."

Again he looked down at the litter, and I touched him. "No . . ."

*"I should have been with you!"* he said angrily. "I went out confident into battle and lost my army. Lost . . ."

I looked down at his wife. "Will she be all right?"

"She will die," he said. "And it is all my fault."

"Nothing is your fault," I replied.

He stared down at the litter, then slowly bent to pick up the poles and drag it into the camp.

THE NEXT MORNING THE SUN PEEKED OVER THE caldera and quickly melted the dusting of snow that had reached up to us. The mountainside was blanketed in clouds below us. The air smelled fresh and cold.

By midday the clouds to the north were gone, giving us a good view of Burroughs. It was a sprawling city, larger than Sagan and Shklovskii put together. There were tall municipal buildings that reminded me of those in Wells. Mining had given Burroughs its wealth. Beyond it, at the northern horizon, was the edge of the polar cap, like a jagged white line of teeth.

"It's magnificent!" I said.

"And dangerous," General Xarr, beside me, added. He looked much the worse for wear. He had spent much of the night with Kerl, getting no sleep. I had not been invited to this particular party; had, with as much politeness as Xarr could muster, been excluded from it.

"I apologize for last night, my lady," Xarr said to me now, by way of explanation. "But Kerl was in need of the company of old military friends and their rum. I hope you understand."

"Of course."

"I do not know much of things other than military," he said, "but I would imagine he will be in need of other company soon."

I regarded the city below.

"What do we need to know about approach?" I asked.

"Well," he began slowly, "to begin with, it is not such a magnificent city as you think. From here, it is pretty and shiny, but it is as corrupt as any other piece of hell. It was built on the blood of men like my ancestors, who came here to get rich and stayed to die poor. A few so-called great men made the city what it is today. The rest were no better than if the F'rar had ruled then."

He paused and stared down at his homeland.

"Today," he went on, "the F'rar are camped to the north. They were driven, so my scouts tell me, out of the city by the initial uprising, but have not left the area. They are about to be joined by a great F'rar army from the west, who began by running like kits but now are organized and on the march again."

"That is the one Newton told me of, with a F'rar named Ceres at its head."

Xarr harrumphed. "I know this Ceres. He is as ruthless as Frane."

Jamie joined us. His haggard look had not abated in the days since I had first seen him again. He looked like an old man in a young body.

"Kerl wishes to see you, my lady."

Jamie stayed behind as I took my leave.

There was a tent set up away from the others, which Kerl had taken for the ministrations of his mate. When I walked in I found Kerl alone, standing over the cushions on which she had been carefully laid. A veil covered her face. She was breathing with difficulty.

"She wants to speak with you," Kerl said as I joined him.

"Is there—"

"There is no hope, and she knows it."

Piesha had turned her head toward us. I could tell she was in great pain. She tried to lift the veil, but her paw could only weakly wave at it.

Gently, Kerl turned the cloth back.

Her face was even more ravaged than it had looked the night before, nearly hairless and horribly scraped, as if claws had dug at her.

"My . . . queen . . ." she said, more weakly than a whisper.

I bent down to her and took her paw in my own. It was lighter than a feather.

"Piesha, don't speak. Save your strength."

"For what?" she asked. "I know I am to die. I have served my clan, my betrothed, and my queen well. . . . But there is something I must say. . . ."

Her head made a motion, and I knelt now to bring my ear close to her lips. "What is it, Piesha?"

"Take . . . care of him . . ." she said. Her grip tightened on my paw. "You must . . . vow . . ."

The words stuck in my throat. "I . . ."

"You must *vow!*" Her voice suddenly strengthened, and she brought her face up to mine. "Please, my queen . . ."

Tears had filled my eyes. "I make that vow to you. . . ."

"Thank you . . ."

She lay back on the pillow, and her breath became very ragged again.

As I stood up beside Kerl, the ragged breathing stopped. He bent down to cover her face again.

"She is gone," he said.

"Did you hear . . ."

"Yes, I heard," he said. His words were so hard-edged that I said nothing.

"Can I spend time with her alone, my queen?" he asked. It was almost a cry of despair.

"Of course."

I left him there, staring down at her, his paws clenched at his sides.

THERE WAS A BURIAL CEREMONY NEAR MIDDAY (I thought of Mighty and his ceremonies) for Piesha and for one of the others who had come in with Kerl during the night and who also had died. It was quick and simple.

Our scouts reported that there was much movement to the west, where Ceres's army had camped a mere twenty kilometers from Burroughs. Unaccountably, the F'rar reinforcements to the north had not moved to join them.

"Perhaps they plan a two-pronged attack on the city, from the north and west?" I asked.

Xarr cleared his throat and replied, "Why even bother with Burroughs? At this point it is of no strategic value. I would have thought Ceres would circumvent it and head south, to Wells."

"He hasn't," Kerl nearly spat, "and that is our problem." He had been more surly than grief-stricken the entire day.

A thought occurred to me: "Ceres has Talon with him."

"Another dust storm machine?" Xarr asked, his eyes widening.

"Or perhaps worse," I answered.

"The only thing to do is to go down into Burroughs and reconnoiter," Kerl said. "Jeffrey of the Science Guild is down there waiting for us with armaments, and I also can draw the rebel forces there into our army. With that added strength, we can destroy the northern forces before they can join Ceres. Then we can sweep east and south, picking up even more forces on the way, and meet Ceres in equal strength before he gets to Wells."

There were no objections to this plan.

"It is late in the day," Xarr commented. I will instruct my spies to prepare your arrival early tomorrow. The rebel forces will be mobilized in Burroughs for you by then."

"Good," Kerl said, banging his paw on the table and then turning angrily to leave.

I caught up with him at the door to the tent. "Talk with me. Let us have a meal."

"I'm not hungry, my queen."

"Then let us walk."

He took a deep breath but then nodded suddenly. "All right," he said.

There was a bluff overlooking the city far below, which had burst out in lights as dusk dropped toward night. It looked like a scattering of stars on the ground. The faraway fires of the mining plants shimmered and danced.

"It is almost beautiful," I said.

"Almost."

I lowered my voice. "Kerl. Look at me."

He did so, though his features were still hard.

"Why are you so angry?"

He looked back at the view and then burst out, "Because I do not grieve for her! I did the same to her that you did to my brother!"

"No one could force you to love her. You know that. She knew that, too."

"But it is still shameful!"

"Yes, it is," I said, awash in my own memories and shame.

The two of us regarded the scene below. A burst of far-away flame from the foundry sent sparks into the sky. I could almost hear them crackle.

"Let me tell you something, Kerl," I said. "A long time ago, when I was betrothed to Kaylan, I locked my heart away. It was as if there was nothing in my chest but an empty place, a hole. And Kaylan knew this. He knew it from the very first time he touched me. And what made it worse was that his own heart was open and unlocked for me. And so the two of us lived with one heart, and it was not enough for love. I was very angry at those who had made me do this to this good man. I think he was angry, too.

"But later, after Kaylan was murdered, I came to understand that for those of us born to duty, there are things more important than our hearts. It is the price we pay to rule. And it is a dear one, as those who do not rule don't always understand.

"And we must pay it, or many thousands, perhaps millions, suffer. It is the sacrifice we make, and we are judged by it. We are, in fact, judged by our actions, not our hearts.

"I think Kaylan, beyond his own pain, knew this, too. I think Piesha knew it. It was the price they paid for duty. And they paid it well."

There were tears in his eyes as he stared straight ahead at the scene below.

"And now—" I began.

He suddenly took me in his arms. "And now we can have our hearts *and* our duty," he said.

"Yes," I answered in a bare whisper. "We are very lucky. And Kaylan and Piesha, I believe, would bless us—"

He kissed me—a kiss I had dreamed about since I was barely older than a kit, and had first seen him laughing with his brother in the grounds outside the palace. They had been playing tag, along with Frane, who kept chasing Kerl. Though Kerl was smaller and younger than his brother, he was quicker and faster. They were both laughing very loud, and then Kerl stopped and looked at me, and our eyes met. . . .

The kiss went on, and on. . . .

"I do wed thee," he whispered in my ear, somewhere in the middle of the night.

"And I thee," I whispered in return, in release.

THE NEXT MORNING, EARLY, KERL AND FOUR GOOD soldiers, including my friend Masie, made ready to go down to Burroughs. It was first light. Each was outfitted with a good horse but little in the way of provisions.

"We will be back by nightfall, with your friend Jeffrey and with an army!" Kerl announced.

Xarr concurred. "Good. We have many plans to make on your return."

"Yes," Kerl said, smiling. He turned to me, and said for everyone to hear, "And a betrothal ceremony among them."

"What's this?" Xarr said in surprise.

"My queen and I are one," Kerl said, grinning. "Last night we made our vows to one another. Tonight we will have the party. Make sure you wear your best available tunic and that the wine steward brings only his best. I will bring more wine and provisions for a party from Burroughs." He shook a bag of money tied to his saddle. "Only the best." He shouted, "Your queen is married!"

There was a cheer from all those awake and nearby.

Kerl locked eyes with me. "Till this evening, my queen."

"Till then," I answered.

"You glow," he said in a lower voice.

I nodded. "I will wait for you to return."

"And I shall hurry!"

He turned his mount, and the four horses began the long, steep climb down the winding switchback trail to the waking city below.

When they had left, I turned to see Xarr's eyes on me, as well as Jamie's. Jamie looked stunned, and the old general had a raffish look on his face.

"So . . ." Xarr said.

"Yes," I answered, and then I laughed.

Xarr turned away. "It's about damned time, my queen."


FOR THE FIRST TIME IN MONTHS THAT SEEMED LIKE years, my heart was as light as those around me. The early scouts reported no movement in either F'rar army, so the day was given over to preparations for my wedding ceremony. I did not believe so much festive bunting could be produced by a traveling army. As if by magic, Brenda and her cohorts produced hunted game ready to be spiced and cooked, and wine long hidden for a special occasion. Though (no surprise!) Massie was also an excellent seamstress, in her stead Bertie, Brenda's husband, did nearly as well. In fact, it was said after he had produced a wedding gown from one of the gaudier tent flaps, that he may even have outdone his rival this time. Though it was stiff and smelled of canvas and harsh weather, it felt like silk and lace to the wearing.

Musicians were produced from among the ranks, and an orchestra of sorts, which started out sounding like sick kits but were more than serviceable by the end of the morning, was assembled and made ready.

I looked forward to this evening as I had never looked forward to any day in my life.

By midafternoon my anticipation had grown to the point where I began to bother Xarr like a child.

At first he laughed, reporting that a rider had reported that an army more than four thousand strong was now on the march to join us and that Kerl was staying behind to round up even more. But late in the day, he had troubling news to impart.

"I don't know what to make of this, my lady," he said. "My scouts report that the F'rar army to the north is pulling far away from the city at great speed."

A bolt of ice went through me. "And Ceres's army?"

"They hold to the west of Burroughs at twenty kilometers. They have been active with their air machines, but only near their camp in maneuvers."

Ten minutes later he came to me with an even deeper frown. "No movements in troops, but our radio machine near Ceres's camp reports from our spy within the F'rar camp that a single airship is headed for Burroughs as of half an hour ago. Perhaps a peace emissary—"

"Get them out!" I shouted, suddenly, intuitively, knowing what was about to happen. "Get Kerl out of the city now!"

Xarr looked at me with confusion. "The army he sent

ahead is just arriving. Kerl should be on his way in an hour or so—"

I found myself crying, which only confused him more. *"Get him out now!"*

"It is imposs—"

It was then I heard the whine of the airship, and ran to the bluff in my wedding gown, now streaking with tears.

The first soldiers of our new army were just making their way into camp, and behind them was a mass of men climbing up the hillside.

At a distant sound, they stopped as one to look at the sky.

*"Kerl!"* I screamed as I saw the tiny dark distant blip approach the city below at a great height. I could imagine my love looking up at it in either comprehension or confusion. *"Oh, my husband!"*

It was then that a flash of light made the day go away. I closed my eyes as the concussion made the ground shake and then roared up the mountainside to hit me with a blast of heated air that knocked me to the ground. At first I could not see and thought I was blind. But I was not. My sight came back, though now I cursed it.

There were cries of alarm around me; the blast of hot wind had torn the party bunting. Now a wall of dust roared up the mountainside, knocking down soldiers like flower petals bent by the wind, and then a cloud engulfed us all. . . .

I AWOKE CHOKING ON DUST. I WAS COVERED HEAD to foot in fine red particles. There was a strange smell in the air, like dried, smoked meat. Around me others were getting to their feet, coughing. Someone was crying. I heard someone hoarsely call my name.

I stood, and brushed myself off as I walked through the settling cloud. I bumped into someone hunched over, retching. It was a soldier, and he looked up at me uncomprehendingly.

"What happened?"

"I don't know," I answered.

The day became brighter as the dust cloud settled: the sun, a dim yellow coin, grew brighter, and now the sky came back. There were high clouds.

I walked to the edge of the bluff and looked down.

I swore: "My creator."

The cloud was settling down the mountainside toward Burroughs, which was still swaddled in dust. As the dust retreated, it revealed an army of men struggling to their feet. They began to trudge sluggishly up the mountainside.

The cloud settled, settled. . . .

I waited for Burroughs to reappear. The dust moved in lessening eddies, clearing away.

There was nothing but a dust-filled crater where the city had been.

"Kerl . . ." I whispered, and knew that he was gone, annihilated, along with Masie and Jeffrey and the many thousands of others who had lived there.

Xarr joined me, wiping his eyes.

"Where . . . ?"

"It's gone. And with it my husband. This was Talon's doing."

A runner covered in dust approached Xarr. "General, the F'rar army to the west is moving. So are the remnants to the north. They are both heading this way, sir."

Xarr stared at him in disbelief.

"Sir . . .?" the runner said, waiting.

I spoke up. "Keep track of their movements. Report any change. I'll need reports on the half hour. Do they have another weapon like the one that was dropped on Burroughs?"

"Our spy in their camp says that was the only one. But they have a tent with parts, possibly for another."

"Very well. Do as I told you."

He stared at me for a moment, then bowed. "Yes, my queen."

He moved off, and I turned to Xarr. There was bitterness and anger in my voice.

"Get the new soldiers organized as fast as you can." I looked out at the place where my husband had died. "Outfit them and organize them. We will destroy Ceres's army before he gets here."

# ⊰ CHAPTER 21 ⊱

I REMEMBER VERY LITTLE MORE ABOUT THAT DAY, EX-
cept for the coppery smell of blood in my nostrils.

We had gained more than four thousand soldiers, and
we used them to good effect. Their thirst for blood was as
great as mine. They had seen their homes and families
wiped from the face of Mars, and they fought with appropriate vigor. Xarr organized them well. But when our
charge down the mountainside toward Ceres's approaching army began, each man and woman heard not the cries
of battle in his ears but the singing of blood lust and
vengeance. I am ashamed to admit I heard the same.

The lower mountain was clothed in a thinning forest of
junto trees. We came screaming out of them like madmen,
a line of four thousand straight at Ceres's army, which had
barely time to organize themselves into ranks. We were
among them before they could react, cutting them to

pieces, driving deep into their numbers. The red earth was stained with red F'rar blood, and my own lungs were hoarse with screaming war cries. At one point I came face to face with Ceres himself, and cut him down without thought, then the F'rar to either side of him and behind. At his end there was only terror in his eyes. The battlefield was littered with bodies like a quarry with stones. Xarr himself reached Talon's tent, where the fat scientist cowered in a corner like a dog. He was taken alive, and told Xarr in a trembling, pleading voice that what had been dropped on Burroughs was a concussion bomb, huge in destructive power. Another lay partly assembled, and he offered it to our use in exchange for his life.

While Xarr was prodding Talon toward me across the battlefield at the point of his sword a group of our new soldiers, natives of Burroughs, spied him, surrounded him, and ran him through repeatedly with their swords. Xarr told me later he could not recall the faces of the men who had done this. I did not press the matter.

And then, finally, as if long years had passed, the cries of battle died out. The sun was low and melancholy on the distant mountains. I sat contemplating my blade, red with drying blood. I felt hollow inside. The countryside was littered with dead F'rar bodies. Their tents had been razed to the ground, their vehicles confiscated or destroyed.

No healthy prisoners were taken—they fought where they stood, or were cut down like wheat before the scythe.

The wounded cried, as if the ground itself were weeping with pain.

Xarr approached me. He was weary with effort, and looked older than the old soldier he was. "There are many wounded F'rar, my lady," he reported. "Shall we put them to the sword?"

I looked up at him and shook my head slowly. "We are not butchers, Xarr. Attend to them."

"But my lady—" He gestured toward the distant ruins of Burroughs.

*"I said we are not butchers!"* Anger rose in me like frustration. "Haven't you seen enough blood today, Xarr? To vanquish the F'rar must we become them?"

He bowed shortly. "As you wish." He moved wearily off, giving orders as he went.

I looked up, and saw that our entire army was facing me where they stood in silence. I tried to focus on them but could not. Then one soldier raised his blade and shouted, "Queen Haydn!" The others followed suit.

Anger and all other feeling drained out of me. I let my blade fall from my grasp, watched its bloodstained edge mingle with the red of the earth. I suddenly felt very weary. My eyes fixed on the blade, and then my vision began to dim, and I could not take my eyes from the red blade. . . .


I AWOKE IN A SUN-DAPPLED TENT, THE SCENT OF fresh flowers caressing my nose. I felt clean and refreshed.

Outside somewhere, a bird trilled happily.

For a moment I thought I had been transported back to my time with Mighty, and when the tent flap was thrown aside for a moment I saw my old friend striding in with purpose, a sly smile redolent of his love of life on his face . . .

It was not Mighty but the cook Brenda who bustled into my tent, letting a bolt of bright daylight in with her before the flap closed coolly behind her again.

"My lady!" she cried happily, moving around me with purpose, fiddling with the huge vase of cut flowers that had been placed on the bedside table. "You're finally awake!"

"How long . . ." My voice was hoarse. I talked in a bare whisper.

"Ah, you'll be needing some gemel tea for your throat, you will." She put her paws on her hips. "You've been asleep for nearly two days, my queen."

"Two—days!"

"Shh, don't be talking, now. I daresay you needed your rest. You'll be needing much more of it for the next two months."

For a moment I stared at her, not understanding—but then reality dawned on me and I fell back against my pillows in disbelief. "You don't—mean—"

"Of course! What else do you think would knock you flat like that? And very much so, according to the doctor."

"A litter . . ."

She was plumping the pillows around me, her own kitcheny scent mixing with that of the flowers.

Suddenly I wanted to throw up.

She helped me with that, laughing as the vase was stripped of its flowers and put to another use.

"I imagine there'll be plenty of that for a few days, too."

"Yes. The last time . . ."

I thought of my first litter. My thoughts went suddenly black. Then I saw Kerl's face, remembered our one night of bliss. Then I was suddenly weeping.

"There, there," Brenda soothed, cradling me against her ample bosom. "You know your condition makes you more weepy, too. It's all right to miss him, lass. He was a good man, but I'm sure his kits will do him proud. In many ways you're a lucky lady. My Bertie and I were never able to have a litter."

I looked up at her, forgetting my tears. "No?"

She rocked me against her. "No. But I'll be here for you the next two months, and so will the rest of us. Nothing will happen to those little ones inside you, lassie. They'll be safe and beautiful as can be."

For a moment I felt real comfort, and then I abruptly yawned.

"Tired again? Ah! Then sleep . . ."

She lay me gently down among the pillows, which cradled me as softly as she had.

"Sleep . . ." I heard her say.

And I did.

AS IT HAD THE FIRST TIME, THE MORNING SICKNESS and weariness quickly passed. This was a good thing, because decisions needed to be made. We had been, on my account, stationary since the battle, and I thought it was time we moved south. Reports were coming in that Wells was in an uproar. Rebels had begun to battle the F'rar openly in the streets, and even Frane, with all of her ruthlessness, was not able to quell them.

Very little stood between us and the capital.

I sat in a cushioned divan in the war tent, feeling very much royal, and Xarr reported, "I estimate we will pick up between six and eight thousand more men on the way to Wells." He pointed to the map spread on the table before us, stabbing a series of towns and small cities on the way down to the capital. He then drew his claw east. "A second, smaller army is forming near Robinson, and will attack Wells from that side while we come in from the north." He circled around to the south. "The trouble is, there is a huge F'rar army moving with speed from Bradbury, and they will get to the city before we do. Even with the reinforcements to the east, we will be outnumbered three to one."

"Then we must find another way to beat them," I said.

"An easy thing to say, my queen. But how?"

I studied the map. "Yes, an easy thing to say . . ."

I looked up at Xarr. "Have we heard from Newton?"

"Nothing. Our radio machines have been trying for days, but there is only silence. A rider is due back late today or tomorrow."

Xarr said, "I hesitate to bring something up, my lady."

"Please do so anyway."

"The . . . concussion device we confiscated from Talon. I'm told it's not far from completion. Perhaps if we threatened Frane with it?"

"Destroy Wells?" I said in disbelief.

"Not Wells, but Frane's hometown of Bradbury."

"Out of the question. I told you before, Xarr: we are not barbarians. It is a monstrous weapon."

"But the threat of it—"

"Would send the city of Bradbury into a panic. And then what if Frane calls our bluff?"

He was silent, his reserves of enlightenment exhausted.

"No, Xarr," I said, softening my tone, "we must find another way."

BUT THAT OTHER WAY ELUDED US. AND THEN IT WAS too late, for on the seventh day of our march south, word came from Xarr's riders and spies that Frane had gathered her army from Bradbury and had swept past Wells, heading straight for us instead. By the time we heard, they were but two days away.

"Instead of defense she has chosen offense," I said. We

had stopped on the plain of Margaritifer Terra the night before and were about to break camp. It was level ground surrounded by rolling hills. I surveyed it, then ordered a halt. "We will stay here and fight."

Xarr waited for me to continue. "Think of it this way, Xarr. If we march, we run straight into Frane in two days. If we stay, and make her come to us, we have an extra day to fortify a battlefield of our own choosing."

"We will still be greatly outnumbered," he said.

"Yes. But we will hold the high ground. What do we know of the F'rar weaponry?"

"Five airships with conventional bombs. All of Talon's toys were concentrated with the western army, so we needn't be concerned with that. You could always make use of that concussion device."

"And forever be known as a butcher in a league with Frane herself? We will not use it, Xarr. We have three days. I suggest we get to work."

"Yes, my queen."

He bowed and left.


IN THREE DAYS WE WERE AS READY AS WE WOULD ever be. Our forces held the high hills surrounding the plain, with a significant line barricaded in the middle of the lowlands facing the one bottleneck opening. The plan was to draw the F'rar army onto the battlefield through this opening, then close it up and tighten the circle around them. We would cut them apart from all sides.

The problem was, our troops were spread very thin, and we had barely enough to do this.

The third day dawned cloudy and bleak, with a chill light rain falling that was as much mist as water. Riders reported the F'rar army a mere two kilometers away, where they had camped.

"They are not taking the bait," Xarr observed at midday when no movement had been reported.

"Then we must sweeten it."

Against Xarr's loud protestations, I chose ten swift riders and mounted my own horse. I wore my best armor, and one of the riders bore a flag of the monarchy, with my family crest, a paw with extended claws clutching a branch of peace.

"If I do not return," I ordered the old general, "do your best without me. Frane will follow me, I'll wager. Whether she will catch me, we shall see."

Without another word, I turned and rode out, leading my little band.

FRANE'S ARMY HAD SETTLED IN A VALLEY BELOW THE third hill to the east. When I topped the rise and looked down on it, at first I saw nothing but a roiling mass in the mist that looked like a live carpet. The valley was filled with F'rar soldiers from end to end. Cook fires were burning here and there.

"Look at them all," my companion bearing the flag marveled.

"Let us hope their blood is up," I said. "Hold that standard high."

He and I rode a bit forward, and he brandished the colors proudly.

I sat straight on my mount and cupped my paws to my mouth, shouting, "F'rar dogs! Have you come to eat, or fight?"

There was a rustle below, and grumble in the near ranks. A few faces turned up to regard us.

"Tell your vile commander, the usurper and traitor Frane, that Queen Haydn has come to put her in her place!"

Now I saw her, the figure of Frane resplendent in bright red robes, making her way out of her tent. Already there was agitated movement at the front of the lines facing me.

To my companions I said, "Be ready to turn and ride like the wind."

I turned around and shouted, "Frane! It is I, Haydn of Argyre, your true queen, who challenges you!"

A few F'rar had mounted horses, and there was a swell of angry churning in the front. An arrow flew past us, close by.

"Chase us, you dogs!"

I took the standard from my carrier and plunged it into the ground in front of me. The angry shouts had turned to a roar. I saw Frane in the midst of it, trying to keep control. By now the rear ranks were moving forward, the cook fires were being trampled out.

A line of riders charged up the hill at us.

I said to my companions: "Now! Ride home with abandon!"

I turned my horse as a splash of bullets hissed past us and a line of arrows flew overhead. Ducking low, I charged to the head of my little column. We raced back west.

Behind us, I counted at least two dozen horses in pursuit, with more in a second line behind them.

"Ride! Ride!" I shouted, driving my mount on, feeling the ground race beneath his hooves.

We topped the second hill as our pursuers gained on us.

I stole a look back and was filled with glee to see what looked to be the entire F'rar army in pursuit behind them.

Down into a short valley I drove, then up again, with my companions keeping pace.

We charged down the last hill and through the bottleneck. I shouted to the startled ranks to either side, "Be awake! They're coming!"

We were through, making for our own lines, which opened in the middle of the field to let us in, closing behind.

The F'rar army charged in a seething mass onto the field of battle, in mad disarray.

The bottleneck closed behind them.

The battle for the control of Mars was joined!

# ⊰ CHAPTER 22 ⊱

IT RAINED, AND THE FIRST NIGHT THE RAIN TURNED TO snow. For a while the snow turned red with blood, and then the snow melted with rising temperatures, carrying the blood into the ground with it. The F'rar attacked and we held, attacked again, and we barely held. Our positions in the hills closed in. But there were just too many of them. By the morning of the second day the F'rar held the high ground to the north and east, and our battle line had been squeezed to the middle of the field, with scant reserves to the west and south.

"They're doing to us what we were going to do to them," Xarr observed.

"Yes," I concurred. "We'll be surrounded before long."

He gave me an estimate of our strength: nearly half dead and wounded.

"It's their damned airships. . . ."

I said nothing, then said, "Continue to do your best."

It was true that their airships, as much as their numerical superiority, had made the difference. From the safety of the sky they had strafed and bombed us, and we had no recourse but luck. We had managed to bring down two of the five with random fire, but the other three had learned to avoid this peril by flying higher, out of range. They were depleting our forces more efficiently than the F'rar ground attacks.

By the end of the second day we were surrounded, with only a quarter of our strength remaining.

It was a starlit night. We lit no fires, because the F'rar airships would use them as night targets. There was sporadic fire, but a kind of truce imposed by darkness had taken effect. The smell from the many F'rar cook fires wafted over our hungry and tired fighters like a pall. I walked through our gloomy camp trying to impart a cheer I did not feel myself. I then joined Jamie in Xarr's tent.

"It occurs to me that they can afford not to fight tonight, because they know that tomorrow they will end it," I said.

Xarr concurred. "There is nothing more we can do. They have only to tighten the noose whenever they want."

Jamie stared gloomily at the ground. I noticed that his paws were shaking.

"Come now, Jamie," I said, forcing myself to sound hearty. "You don't fear death, do you?"

"Do you?" he said, looking up at me. He looked like a haunted man.

"Of course I do. I fear for my litter more than for myself. And I fear for my people."

He nodded, trembling, and looked at the ground again. "I fear only one thing, my lady: that the legitimate queen of Mars will not be returned to the throne."

Patiently waiting out this scene, Xarr said to me, "At first light they will commence attacks from the air. Then they will make a final charge."

"Yes," I answered.

"And, of course, they will put us to the sword."

"That will be Frane's way."

"She may . . . want to take you alive, my queen. That would not be pleasant. If you would prefer . . ." He brushed the hilt of his sword with his claws, not looking away.

"It would be better for all of us, I think. Thank you, General."

"And you, Jamie?" Xarr asked, trying to lighten his voice in grim jest. "Would you like me to run you through, too, like a chicken on a spit?"

Jamie ignored him, continuing to stare at the ground.

Xarr mused, "It is a quick end for such a long enterprise."

"If it must end, let it end with us fighting for what is just."

We stood silently, lost in our own thoughts.


DAWN ROSE, GLORIOUS YELLOW AND PINK, AND, AS Xarr had predicted, their airships went to work on us. We had retreated into a tight little force, less than a thousand within a circle of fortifications. For them, it was like dropping stones into a barrel. They went about their work with élan.

Near midday, I watched as Frane's army made ready to overrun us. I could see her, a far spot of brilliant red, redder than blood, moving her troops into position. The airships circled above, ready to attack like killing hawks. . . .

And then, in the hush before this final assault, there was a sound below and beyond all other sounds: a deep droning that grew and grew in the west. The airships overhead pulled up and away. And then, as if by magic, I saw one of them give a cough, there was a puff of smoke, and it dropped like a dead bird to the ground between us and the F'rar army. The other two fled to the east—and then a massive black machine soared overhead, sleek as a bird, screaming an anger that roared against the sky. It followed the remaining two F'rar machines, dropping them from their perches in the clouds. We saw two bursts of black smoke where the airships had been and then the gargantuan bird turned and began to drop scorching swaths of fire on the F'rar lines.

There was chaos in front of us. I shouted, "Charge them!" and our small and tired army, suddenly energized and filled with hope, climbed our barricades and made for the scattered F'rar ranks.

Behind us I heard a war cry. I turned in wonder to see rank upon rank of reinforcements, well armed and disciplined, rushing to join us. At their head was the pirate Pelltier, who swept up beside me on his horse, smiling hugely. "Girlie!" he shouted, doffing his cap, and then he rode by, pulling his sword from its sheath and wading into the chaotic mass of F'rar. I spurred my mount and followed.

The giant airship drew away after decimating the enemy lines, and left the rest of it to us on the ground. We made quick work of them. I saw a bright patch of red in the middle of the fray and made my way steadily toward it, fighting as I went.

When I reached it I found Frane's blood-red cloak hanging empty on a spear mounted tightly in the ground.

"Frane!" I shouted. "Show yourself, usurper!"

Around me the battle wound down. Xarr rode up with an exultant, flushed look on his old face.

"It was a miracle!" he cried.

"Even better than one. It was the Science Guild." I gave him orders for organizing prisoners, of whom there were hundreds, if not thousands. "Remember," I reminded him, "put no one to the sword."

Then I rode to the rear to find, as I expected, my friend Newton.

He had landed his monstrous black flying machine in the valley behind our lines, and was studying its back end, which was composed of two huge round ports.

"Now you know what we do in our cellars," he greeted me, smiling. He pointed to the west, where a second flying ship lay nestled beside a third.

I embraced him with an enthusiasm that startled him. "You saved us. You saved the monarchy!"

"I heard about Talon's weapon at Burroughs, and Kerl and Jeffrey," he said, unsmiling. "I only wish we had arrived sooner."

"What's done is done."

"You are with kit?" he asked, the amused, ironic tone returning to his voice. "This is what I hear."

"I am."

"Is Frane captured?"

"No. But we will hunt her like a dog."

He snorted. "Apt. What will you do now?"

"March on Wells."

"There is no need. Wells is free of the F'rar. There is celebration in the streets as we speak."

My head was reeling from the events of the past hours. "How did you get Pelltier to help?"

Newton smiled. "I asked! He is a rogue, but a steadfast and true one. He believes in what you are doing. The rest, for him, was easy. He has raised armies before, when necessary. And besides, he likes you."

I laughed. "The last time I saw him, he offered to buy me from Jeffrey for his whorehouse."

Newton answered, "He has a whorehouse, Haydn. But he meant to buy you for his *wife*."

I said nothing, and then we both laughed.

I WAS STUNNED BY THE EVENTS THAT HAD TAKEN place on the very eve of our destruction. Now a kind of ennui set in. It had much to do with the litter I bore, I knew. When the adrenaline was needed for battle, the body supplied it; but now that the battle was won, my kits took all my energy, leaving little for me.

I was carried into Wells in triumph, and the sight of the old city caused tears to come to my eyes. Though its skyline had been altered by the F'rar destruction, its heart had not, and the people welcomed me back with what a fool might call love. Whatever it was—relief, patriotism, nostalgia for the past—I knew I had much work to do, and that it must be done quickly.

A week after my return, when the celebrations had died down, I called Newton, Xarr, and Jamie to counsel and put the question to them:

"How long must I rule until I can reinstate the Republic?"

Jamie blurted: "It is impossible for you to even think about it at this point! There are still minor rebellions in some of the outlying cities. The people would fear another coup. Frankly, so do I!"

Xarr said, "These so-called rebellions are little more than local disturbances over disruption of services and trade. They were caused as much by the F'rar as by the rebellion against them. A few local leaders have been jailed over the ... let us say, vociferousness of their protest. These protests are diminishing. I would counsel a cautious approach to reinstatement of the Republic at this point, but only because I am a cautious man. Too much change in too little time can be disruptive in itself."

Newton said, choosing his words carefully, "You already know my opinion, my lady. The Republic cannot return too soon for me."

I noted his ironic smile and the twinkle in his eye as I answered. "I tend to agree with Newton. Whatever the consequences, the Republic should be reinstated with all speed."

Jamie, much agitated, said, "Can I counsel that my queen wait until the new council chambers are completed in the spring? It is only five weeks away. You will have your kits by then, and the people will be used to new ideas again. It will take months just to organize elections, after the chaos the F'rar imposed. And speaking of the F'rar—"

"They will be represented in the new government," I announced simply.

Jamie was startled, and so, I saw, was Xarr. Only Newton retained his bemused look.

"That is impossible!" Jamie protested. "That declaration alone would cause renewed fighting in the streets!"

"They must be represented," I answered, "or there will never be stability. They are the largest and most powerful clan on Mars, too large to ignore. The leaders of their recent usurpation, including and especially Frane, must be caught and brought to justice, but after that the F'rar must be represented."

"It was the mistake your father made!" Jamie began bitterly.

"We will not make the mistake this time of allowing one group to dominate the Assembly. I am working on safeguards to prevent this."

I noted the broadening of Newton's wry smile. We had already had many talks about this, and I looked forward to many more. "You must realize, Jamie, and you too, Xarr, that great scientific changes are coming. We must be ready for them, and institute them for the good of our people. As Newton has informed you, our planet may be slowly losing its atmosphere. For this reason alone we need unity, to combat it. The Republic I envision is not the one that was so recently overthrown. It will be stronger, and even more representative."

Jamie was about to speak but I held up my hand, suddenly tired.

"We will speak of these things again. I'm afraid I must rest now."

The meeting was adjourned, but Jamie, as I expected, stayed behind.

Laying back on my pillow, half closing my eyes, I smiled at my old page. "I know how you feel," I said, feeling even more tired than I had a moment before. "Believe me, I've always known how you feel. But I believe in my heart that I am on the right course."

"Your father was a fool, but not a complete one," Jamie said. He could not hide the bitterness in his voice. "He knew as soon as he declared the Republic that he had made a mistake. But by then it was too late. It is the *monarchy* that will bring stability to the planet. Do you really think the people have changed all that much since the recent F'rar atrocities that they are ready for self-determination again?"

"All I can say is that I hope so," I replied. "It has been my belief from the beginning."

There was silence, and I opened my eyes to see Jamie glaring at me, his paws clenched. He turned and stalked out of the room.

"My queen, I fear you are a bigger fool than your father."

I lay back and let out a long breath. I could feel the stirrings of life within me. One of the kits—I was sure there were at least two—gave me a kick that almost tickled.

I gave a short laugh.

"I will see you before too long, little one," I whispered, feeling the cool breeze of the afternoon wash over me from the open window. I was drifting off to sleep, and it felt like luxury. "And then perhaps you and I will make them all understand."

# ⇥ CHAPTER 23 ⇤

IT WAS A GLORIOUS SPRING. PERHAPS THE CREATOR had looked down on us and seen us a good people, worthy of beauty and trust. Or perhaps, as Newton claimed, always in his wry, fatherly way, we were lucky with meteorological patterns and would doubtless be unlucky again in future springs.

Whatever the cause, I reveled in it. This litter, I found, was much harder to carry than the first. Also, I was not as young as I had been. I felt weary much of the time, and was confined to bed for long stretches. Also, due to Newton's scolding, I gave up my precious cigarettes. But the glorious weather—cool, fresh mornings, a light, warm wind in the afternoons carrying the scent of blooming flowers, followed by windless cool nights resplendent with stars—made the lassitude not only bearable but also enjoyable. I felt almost like a kit myself again.

Work on the new Hall of Assembly was going splendidly. On days when I did feel up to travel I allowed myself to be transported the short distance to the site and watch the work commence. The new building, of pink sandstone, was covered by a web of scaffolding, but one could see it taking shape: a tall, plain, proud structure, devoid of ornamentation save for the edifice itself, which would end at its apex with a point. In symbolism, it would point "To the heavens and to the future." These words, and none other, would be carved above its doors.

Since work had now risen above the intervening rooftops, on days when I could not visit I could now watch the progress from my own window. It would not be long before that finishing spire was set in place, and the Second Republic of Mars could be declared.

I had spent nearly all of my intervening time on the declaration I would make in just weeks. I had decided that on the very day of my coronation, I would dissolve the monarchy. It would be a fitting end and a fitting beginning. After much consultation and thought, I had decided that the seeds of destruction of the first Republic lay in its very formation. A hall of squabbling senators could never rule effectively, but they could rule as *part* of a government, as one arm held in check by others. I contemplated an Assembly of the People, which would break the rule of the clans by circumventing its leaders. Only common citizens could be elected to it by other common citizens from their own region. In addition, there would be a single minister with little power save over the two governing bodies. This minister would be in effect a referee. It was a fascinating concept, and I spent most of my waking hours refining it.

• • •

WHILE DOING SO ONE FINE DAY IN OUR FINEST OF
springs, I was visited in the queen's chamber by Pelltier
the pirate.

I nearly burst into laughter when, after being announced, he entered. He was dressed in a ridiculous getup,
his or someone else's idea of formal clothes. I had never
met a man, except perhaps Mighty, who was less disposed
toward formal attire.

I could not help a single blurt of laughter, which made
him frown.

"You don't approve, no?" he asked. He could barely
move his neck in the high collar he wore, over a stiff white
shirt and brown breeches that looked newly woven, they
were so stiff. Even his boots looked new and uncreased by
wear.

"Who dressed you?"

He scowled. "I dress myself, my lady." He bowed. "I
also vow never to call you my girlie again."

He blushed, and I was so touched that my own wish to
make fun of him vanished.

"What is it I can do for you today, Pelltier?" A waft of
flower-scented breeze washed over me, making me languidly sleepy.

"You work?" he said, pointing to the documents on the
table before me and advancing in a stiff way.

"Yes, I work. Why don't you remove those ridiculous
boots?"

"He tell me I must dress like a gentleman to see the
queen."

"Who is 'he'?"

"The man he sell me dese clothes!"

I smiled. "Well, Pelltier, it seems that for the first time
in your life you have been pirated."

He cocked his head, thinking, and then burst out laughing: "My lady is right! I am robbed!"

With a scoffing motion, he unbuttoned the top of his collar and sat down on the floor. With some effort, he pulled off his boots.

"That is much better!" he said with relief when he was done.

"I want to thank you for all your help at the Battle of Bradbury," I said.

He stood, breathing easier, and waved a hand in dismissal. "That is nothing. I do it for you and would do it again. You are my queen. And . . ."

"Yes?"

He suddenly fell to one knee. "And I ask you for betrothal!"

I must have blinked, startled, because his face locked with determination and he crawled forward on his knees, holding his paws out. "Betroth me, my queen!"

"Pelltier, stand up!" I sputtered, trying to make it sound like a royal command.

He stood up quickly, nearly at eye level with me now. His face looked tortured and confused. "No woman has ever done these things to me before! No woman has ever made me want to give up piracy and live as her complete slave!"

"Pelltier!"

"I do not care if you know it—if the world knows it! I, Pelltier, love you, my queen! I would raise your kits as my own, and love them as much as I love you! I have felt this way always!"

I had recovered somewhat. I bade him sit down, which he did. I reclined in my chair, feeling very much tired.

Pelltier must have noticed this because he rushed to me, his face flushed with concern.

"Are you all right, my lady?"

"Yes, Pelltier. Please, sit back down and we will talk."

He did so, and began talking himself. "Pelltier is so confused, my lady! Ever since I see you again, on the field of battle, my mind is twirling like a child's top! You must give me your answer!"

"I will give you my answer, Pelltier," I said calmly, "but first I must tell you that when I first met you I completely misunderstood your intentions. I thought you wanted me for one of your . . ." I waved my hand, trying not to say the word.

He barked a sudden laugh. "Ha! You think I want you for a concubine! This is foolish!"

"Yes, it is foolish, but it is what I thought. And now we have just met again recently, and I realize my mistake, and I now understand your intentions . . ." Again I waved my hand, and suddenly his frown went away and he nodded.

"Ah, I see! The lady does not wish to betroth her Pelltier!"

I said gently, "Actually, that is true . . ."

"I see! Very well!" He stood up briskly. I thought he was angry, but there was a look almost of relief on his face. "Then I am free to go?"

"Of course you are free to go! Why wouldn't you be?"

"If the lady had accepted my proposal, then Pelltier would have had to stay here, in the city of Wells, forever! And it would unman him!"

"But I thought—"

He bowed. "The lady will always be in my heart! This will not change." When he looked up, his eyes were hard and firm. "I would do anything for you, my lady, anything to protect you. Pelltier will always feel this way. But now, after the ceremonies, I will return to the places I love, in the northwest."

Sensing his seriousness and the burdens of his heart, I did not smile, and I bowed my head. I hoped I looked regal.

"Pelltier is a good servant and a good man. And I am only sorry that my heart was not in the same place as his."

He bowed again. "Thank you, my lady."

He backed out of the room, spying his boots and then scuttling forward to grab them. As he got to the door he turned his head up to me and smiled mischievously. "And now I shall visit that tailor, my lady," he said with a wink, and withdrew.

I lay back, exhausted.

I could not wait for the moment of my coronation, so that I could immediately renounce it, and with it all the ceremony such as I had just endured.

# ⊰ CHAPTER 24 ⊱

**FINALLY, THE DAY OF MY KITS' BIRTHING ARRIVED.**
I was confined to bed for the entire last week, which
came as a relief of sorts. Jamie and my other advisers handled much of the day-to-day work, leaving me free to
watch the completion of the new Hall of Assembly from
my window. Fittingly, the pointing spire was mounted on
the very morning of the day I gave birth to my beautiful
son and daughter.

Sebastian, named after Johann Sebastian Bach, the Old
One composer in Newton's book, came first, and, by order
of succession, this cursed him in my mind because, by rule
of monarchy, he was firstborn. And then my little Amy,
named for Amy Beach, came. Compared to the littering,
the births were easy, and afterward, as I listened to their
sweet, mewling cries, I entered into a swoon such as I had
never known, a dreamy place of serenity and contentment

where the problems of my world receded to nonexistence. One of the nursemaids told me that I had muttered Kerl's name in my half sleep, and this may very well have been so. I resided in a sort of nirvana for a time, all of my memory's making, where my mother held me and my father beamed down on me with his stern wisdom, and all of the loves of my life stood around about me as I held my two new kits. I awoke from this half dream to see that it was true to the extent that my two kits were swaddled beside me, clean and looking slick as little monkeys, their tiny pinched faces closed with slumber. I held them so close that I felt their tiny ticking heartbeats. For a while the contentment of my dream was made real.

They grew strong, and so did I. I awoke one late morning three days after the birth to see Jamie in my chamber, standing mesmerized over the two kits in their matching bassinets. There was such a look of astonishment, almost awe on his features that I startled him with my laugh.

He turned, apologizing. "I'm sorry—"

"They won't bite, you know, if you want to pick one up."

"Which one is Sebastian?" he said in a low voice filled with wonder.

I laughed again. "The one with the male appendage, if you want to peek beneath the swaddling." He flushed so readily that I instantly apologized, then asked, "Why is it that you were never betrothed, Jamie?"

"I never had the time to look for a mate," he said in all seriousness. He was still staring at the two kits, and I said, "Sebastian has a tiny streak of black in the white fur of his crown. His sister does not."

He bent over to examine each, then gently picked up one of the kits, holding it like fine china.

"Sebastian . . ." he whispered.

"Yes."

A nursemaid scuttled in and, scolding, took the kit from Jamie, placing it back in its bassinet. "The queen needs her rest, and so do the little ones!" she announced.

"Of course," Jamie said, backing away.

"Is there something you needed to talk about?" I asked.

"Yes," he said, looking preoccupied. "It can wait."

"Is it about the ceremony? I will be ready for it next week."

"I'm sure you will, my queen. I will come back when you are stronger."

But I was already drifting off back to my dreamful slumber.

A WEEK LATER I WAS READY. THE DAY CAME WITH another glorious dawn, but the weather turned by midday, and then a spring rain came, insistent but light with the scent of wet flowers and the season itself.

The skies had darkened, but my mood had not. In hours I would be crowned queen, and then, moments later, be free of it. This thought alone filled me with my former strength.

Jamie came to see me just after my dressing. The gown was ridiculous and gaudy, all white lace and a flowing train meters long; I was afraid someone else if not myself would trip on it, and had bunched it up at my feet like a brooding pet while I went over the words of my declaration one final time.

"It is very strong," Jamie said as he entered, and I did not look up.

"I know it is. I hope you approve of the changes?"

There was silence, so I looked up. Jamie stood there holding a tray.

"I meant the gemel tea," he said.

"Oh!" I said with a laugh, and put down my pen. "Put it here, and drink with me before we go out together."

"Very well." He looked older, more somber than ever.

Taking a deep breath, I pushed my document aside.

He put down the tray and drew two cups of steaming tea from the single pot, and pushed one across to me. "As I said, it is very strong."

"I'm sure it is." I lifted the hot liquid and sipped, then sipped again.

I looked up over the rim of the cup to see Jamie staring at me with a mixed look of horror and exultation.

"It is done, then," he said in a whisper.

"Wha—"

But I did not finish my word, for a familiar feeling of panic and freezing terror overcame me. My throat constricted, and then I smelled the odor that should have warned me, the same that had tickled my nostrils when Mighty's concubine Hera had tried to assassinate me.

"This time it is *very* strong," Jamie said. "You will die."

My eyes must have held the question my lips could not speak. For as I slowly collapsed to the floor, Jamie came around the table and stood over me.

"*Why,* you ask? Don't you know why, Haydn?" His eyes were filled with tears while his voice rose. "Because you will not be queen! Because everything we worked for, *I* worked for, would be destroyed if you went out there today! The monarchy is the only hope for Mars, and you would have destroyed it! And though I loved you, *I could not let that happen!* Just as I could not let it happen when your father threw it away." He bent closer. "He paid, too, at my hand. I thought they would immediately crown you after the assassination, but the fools tried to carry on the Republic, even as Frane's threat was building! Everything I've done, I've done for the true monarchy. It is all that counts!"

Howling in rage, he stood straight, drew his own full cup, and held it up. "They will come now, and crown you before you die, and then your son Sebastian will be king and"—he drank the entire cup of deadly tea down in a gulp and then held the cup higher in salute—*"long live the monarchy!"*

Screaming with sudden agony, he collapsed atop me even as the room was filled with others. . . .

I AWOKE IN A HAZE OF PAIN. I STILL COULD NOT speak, but I could hear what sounded like a hive of buzzing insects. I could not move my legs or arms, or feel them.

"She is awake!" someone said. I saw Xarr's face come very close to mine, and then Newton's grim visage. Then I saw Pelltier's tear-streaked face.

"I have run the traitor through with my own sword, my lady, to make sure his death."

His face withdrew. Someone behind him held something on a pillow—a delicate gold crown tipped with tiny red rubies. It looked as light as spun glass—and as heavy as the lead of death itself.

I tried to speak but could not utter a word nor move a muscle.

The crown was placed on my head, and words spoken.

Then it was removed. I saw it carried on its pillow by its bearer, who stood waiting between the two bassinets.

I thought of how heavy that crown would lie on my poor son's head, what a curse had befallen him.

"Sebastian . . ." I said, in a whisper behind unmoving lips.

And then I said no more.

Fantasy that *Goes* to the
Next Millennium and Beyond

# Flights
## edited by Al Sarrantonio
0-451-45977-6

This daring, all-new anthology showcases some
of the genre's biggest names and hottest
newcomers. Setting the standard for the
twenty-first century, this collection presents
fantasy that rocks the field of
science fiction.

Includes new stories from:
**Neil Gaiman**
**Harry Turtledove**
**Dennis L. McKiernan**
**Joyce Carol Oates**
**Orson Scott Card**
**And others**

**Available wherever books are sold or at
www.penguin.com**

A444

# Penguin Group (USA) Inc. Online

*What will you be reading tomorrow?*

Tom Clancy, Patricia Cornwell, W.E.B. Griffin,
Nora Roberts, William Gibson, Robin Cook,
Brian Jacques, Catherine Coulter, Stephen King,
Dean Koontz, Ken Follett, Clive Cussler,
Eric Jerome Dickey, John Sandford,
Terry McMillan…

You'll find them all at
**http://www.penguin.com**

*Read excerpts and newsletters,
find tour schedules, and enter contests.*

Subscribe to Penguin Group (USA) Inc. Newsletters
and get an exclusive inside look
at exciting new titles and the authors you love
long before everyone else does.

**PENGUIN GROUP (USA) INC. NEWS**
http://www.penguin.com/news